MADEMOISELLE BAMBÙ

MADEMOISELLE BAMBÙ

PIERRE MAC ORLAN

ILLUSTRATIONS BY **GUS BOFA**

TRANSLATED BY **CHRIS CLARKE**

WAKEFIELD PRESS

CAMBRIDGE, MASSACHUSETTS

Published in French as *Mademoiselle Bambù*
© Éditions Gallimard, Paris, 1982
This translation © 2017 Wakefield Press
Illustrations by Gus Bofa © 2017 Artists Rights Society (ARS), New York / ADAGP, Paris
Ouvrage publié avec le concours du Centre national du livre.

Wakefield Press, P.O. Box 425645,
Cambridge, MA 02142

This book was set in Garamond Premier Pro
Abadi MT Condensed Extra Bold, and
Helvetica Neue LT Pro by Wakefield Press.
Printed and bound in the United States of America.

ISBN: 978-1-939663-25-2

Available through D.A.P./Distributed Art Publishers
75 Broad Street, Suite 630
New York, New York 10004
Tel: (212) 627-1999
Fax: (212) 627-9484

10   9   8   7   6   5   4   3   2   1

CONTENTS

TRANSLATOR'S INTRODUCTION

"What a writer needs is a past," said Pierre Mac Orlan to Raymond Queneau in May of 1960, "and even better, a past that weighs heavily upon him."[1] Mac Orlan's formative decades were filled with enough misery and adventure for his taste, carrying him from the streets of Paris in the opening decade of the new century to the fronts of the First World War and around Europe. It was this cumbersome past that permitted Mac Orlan to spend the next five decades of his life as a passive adventurer, the sort of imagination-based traveler he so poignantly described in his *Handbook for the Perfect Adventurer* (1920).[2]

"The only thing of which I am at all sure," stated Mac Orlan during a television interview with André Gillois in 1957, "is that I was born in Péronne, the 26th of February 1882."[3] Pierre Dumarchey, later to be known as Pierre Mac Orlan, spent his first years in the Somme department of northern France, a decade after the end of the Franco-Prussian War. His mother having passed in 1889, Pierre and his brother Jean were sent to be raised and tutored by their uncle in Orléans. Pierre finished high school before heading off to Rouen, where he was to study to be a teacher. His relationship with his uncle was always difficult and eventually grew untenable; at seventeen, the young Dumarchey withdrew from school and made his way to Paris to become an artist. After a trying first few years in Paris, in the spring of 1902 Pierre returned to Rouen, where he worked doing corrections in a printer's shop.[4] During this time he learned to play the accordion and honed his skills as a painter, illustrator, and writer. Although the reasons and dates are uncertain, it is clear that he was back and forth between Paris and Rouen until 1905, at which time he left Rouen to complete his mandatory military service.

Later in life, Mac Orlan burned a large quantity of his early correspondence, wanting to avoid "posthumous concerns," as he put it. According to Daniel Morcrette, a rare book dealer who was present at one of these "cleansings," "[Mac Orlan] flung letters from Apollinaire and Colette into the furnace with a true appearance of joy." Much of the personal and social mythos that resurfaces time and time again in Mac Orlan's work originates in the murky shadows of the first decade of the twentieth century. It is difficult to determine with any precision the adventures and personal tragedies that befell Pierre in this formative period, and Mac Orlan's clear desire to leave those years behind the curtain where they lay has only exacerbated the vagueness of the era. As Jean-Claude Lamy puts it,

> The novelist was worried that the puzzle that was his life would be too easily put back together. The missing pieces would protect him from the indiscreet curiosity of posterity. He wanted to forget Pierre Dumarchey and erase all trace of his passage. Only Pierre Mac Orlan counted, a name he had made for himself."[5]

Of the puzzle pieces we have from this period, some come from Mac Orlan himself, others from his contemporaries. One foundational episode took place in Rouen toward the end of 1901. It involves an encounter with a mysterious vagabond who went by the name of Star, a supposed seafarer of Dutch origin who was involved in "every twist and turn of the nocturnal side of Rouen."[6] One evening saw Pierre, Jean, Star, and others aboard a small boat in the Seine; an altercation between a drunken Jean and the mysterious Star ended with Jean violently and repeatedly striking Star in the head with an oar. Jean ended up in the river. The incident left Pierre looking over his shoulder for some time, and Jean fleeing Rouen for Barcelona, where, "running out of resources and sought by the police, he enlisted in the Foreign Legion."[7] Star, this unsavory adventurer, would reappear in the works of Mac Orlan on several occasions, and can be seen behind the masks of Jean Mac Guldy in *La Maison du Retour Écoeurant* (1912) [The House of the sickening return] and Captain Hartmann in *Mademoiselle Bambù*.

Another formative event in Mac Orlan's early life involved travels undertaken as secretary to a wealthy Belgian writer, a woman whose identity remains lost in Mac Orlan's hazy past.[8] His duties, by Nino Frank's account, were to correct and recopy his employer's writings. In the company of this unidentified author, the young Mac Orlan traveled to Italy and Belgium, with stops in Naples, Palermo, and Bruges, spending parts of 1907 with her in her rural villa outside the Flanders town of Knokke. Other than this voyage, most of Mac Orlan's early insight into foreign lands and the vagabond's life came second-hand from his brother Jean, who had reenlisted in the Foreign Legion in 1909 after an abbreviated stint with the French infantry stationed at Arras. During these years, Jean Dumarchey took part in campaigns in Algeria, Morocco, and finally Tonkin, in northern Vietnam. Jean died from a head injury immediately after the First World War.

By 1908, Pierre Mac Orlan was back in Paris, and spent much of his time in Montmartre, a regular patron of bars such as Au Lapin Agile behind Sacré Coeur and the Criterion Bar near Saint-Lazare. There he came to know writers such as Guillaume Apollinaire, Francis Carco, and Léon-Paul Fargue, as well as artists and musicians, among them Henri de Toulouse-Lautrec, Pablo Picasso, and Aristide Bruant. Apollinaire, whom

Mac Orlan had first met during the winter of 1903 at the Lapin Agile, lived a short walk from the apartment where Mac Orlan would settle after his return. He would immortalize Mac Orlan's apartment in his *Le Flâneur des deux rives* (1918):

> This is the home of Monsieur Pierre Mac Orlan, that merry author with his imagination full of cowboys and soldiers of the Foreign Legion. There is nothing remarkable about the exterior of the house where he lives. But should you enter, you will come upon a labyrinth of halls, of stairs, of courtyards, and of balconies, so maze-like that it can be rather difficult to find one's way. Monsieur Pierre Mac Orlan's door can be found at the end of the darkest hall in the building. The apartment itself is furnished with a rich simplicity. Many books, but very well chosen. A stuffed woolen guard stands watch, his attitude and position varying along with the moods of his house's master. Above the mantle in the main room hangs a very small caricature of me drawn by Picasso. Large windows open onto a wall situated some ten feet away, and, if you lean out a bit, to your left you will see the gasometers, their altitude never the same as when last you looked, and, to your right, the rails of the train tracks. At night, the six gigantic chimneys of the gas plant flame away magnificently: the color of the Moon, the color of blood, green flames or blue flames. O Pierre Mac Orlan, how Baudelaire would have loved the singular mineral landscape you have discovered hidden away in Auteuil, a neighborhood known for its gardens![9]

During the years immediately following his return to Paris, Mac Orlan subsisted from the meager returns of his art, short radio pieces, songs, and from the writing of erotica. He penned no fewer than thirteen of these "bottom-shelf novels" between 1908 and 1914, and three more in the years that followed the war. A number of these were "legitimate" publications by Jean Fort, a publisher and bookseller, while others were clandestine and sold by subscription.[10] In an unusual twist, many of the books published by Fort did not appear under a pseudonym as one might expect, but are instead, along with several of the songs from this era, among the few works signed by the name Pierre Dumarchey. According to Mac Orlan's friend Pascal Pia, when he inquired as to why Mac Orlan signed much of the erotica he had written under the name Dumarchey, he explained that it was to annoy his uncle, who had been so hard on him in his youth.[11]

Like Blaise Cendrars, Mac Orlan would leave behind poetry in the early 1920s, and focus almost exclusively on prose, privileging fiction and the essay. The one exception to this, of course, was his continued interest in the popular song. But it was a decade earlier, in the apartment on Rue du Ranelagh, that Mac Orlan would make his first foray into the literary novel with *La Maison du retour écoeurant*. Published in 1912, this nonsensical adventure novel would later have an impact on younger writers such as Raymond

Queneau and Boris Vian. Queneau would join Mac Orlan on the Académie Goncourt jury, being elected a year after him in 1951, while all three would be members of the Collège de 'Pataphysique (although Mac Orlan would not join until nine years after Vian's untimely death). Like many of his subsequent titles, *La Maison du retour écoeurant* featured a cover illustration by Gus Bofa, whom Mac Orlan had met in 1910 through fellow illustrator Chas Laborde. Bofa was then editor-in-chief of *Rire*, and although Bofa declined the illustrations Mac Orlan brought him, he suggested that in their place Mac Orlan write humorous tales for the magazine.[12] Mac Orlan would continue to paint and draw for a few more short years, but it was around the time of his introduction to Bofa that he turned to writing full time, launching a career as a writer that would last six decades. As Bofa put it, "Writing is for Mac Orlan (as painting is for certain artists, Pascin for example, and perhaps Grosz) a means of ridding himself, via a semblance of realization, of the more troubling elements of the subconscious mind, which are of no use to him during his 'normal' life."[13]

Mac Orlan also worked in journalism, and from an early age he took an active interest in photography. As a journalist, he covered boxing, rugby, and the Tour de France; he was sent to interview Mussolini in 1925; and in 1932 he wandered the streets of prewar Berlin in the company of George Grosz, writing a series of articles for *Paris-Soir.* His involvement with photography and his association with the practitioners of this young art led to his being invited to provide introductions to the early books of many of his talented contemporaries. He prefaced Germaine Krull's work in 1931, and provided the text for *Paris Seen by André Kertész* in 1934. "Photography," wrote Mac Orlan in his monograph on Eugène Atget that same year, "makes use of light to study shadow. It reveals the people of the shadows. It is a solitary art in the service of the night." For Mac Orlan, the photograph brought about death for a single instant; it afforded a perception of the fantastic that was invisible during everyday life. This sensibility fueled his writing, and these fleeting images stolen from time became instrumental in the development of his aesthetic.

This "picturesque," as he would often describe it, as atemporal as it could seem, was firmly anchored in the anxiety of the new century. Mac Orlan's response to the fantastic elements of the literary generation that had preceded him was decidedly contemporary, fueled by the rapidly evolving city and a social anarchy and despair that was palpable in the streets during the years leading up to the Great War. For Mac Orlan, there wasn't always a need for the out-and-out fantastic so treasured by the likes of Jean Lorrain or Remy de Gourmont; the unknowable depths of the human individual and the chaos of the everyday provided more than enough darkness and suspense.

Mac Orlan's personal conception of this aesthetic continued to develop throughout his career, and these threads, some more pronounced than others, run through his entire oeuvre, from his early poetry and *poésie documentaire* ("documentary poetry") to his fiction, his reportage, and even his writing on photography. His exploration of this emerging postsymbolist and prewar (and later interwar) Europe took shape in poems like "Simone de Montmartre," in novels such as *La cavalière Elsa* (Elsa the cavalier), *Malice*, and *La Vénus internationale* (The Venus international). He would eventually describe this aesthetic as *le fantastique social*, or "the social fantastic." From these novels of the early 1920s, the social fantastic would stretch itself out with shadowy fingers through the rest of his career, lending its anxiety to works such as *Quai des brumes* (1927), *La Tradition de minuit* (1930), and *Mademoiselle Bambù*. To this exploration within his fiction, Mac Orlan added several volumes' worth of essays, some of which would later be collected as *Aux Lumières de Paris* (1925) and *Chroniques de la fin d'un monde* (1925). Not only Paris but Western Europe (and in particular, its ancient port cities) would be as sinister an actor in these works as any other player, its uncertain future inscribed in a hazy map of its labyrinthine streets and seedy underbellies read by the dim light of a glowing tobacco pipe.

In 1925, he shared his vision of this new literary landscape in *La Lanterne sourde* (The muted lantern), a short book of essays, the title of which is an unmistakable nod to Jules Renard: "In a few years, one of our bolder publishers, dragged along by the demands of the public, will compose the first chapter of a long-preordained novel, fashioned out of colored lights atop the roof of a building on Rue Pigalle or in one of the Grands Boulevards. The sky will become an immense book where the unavoidable phrases of an advertisement will be inscribed in flamboyant letters. This has already come to pass. The night's somber veil covers only those few remaining neighborhoods where commerce takes place during the day, and the night is left to sleeping."[14] These were the twin Europes that Mac Orlan saw superimposed one atop the other: the first as illusory as it was respectable, illuminated by daylight, commerce, and tradition; the other equal parts malevolent and honest, peopled by all manner of men and women: thieves, soldiers and mercenaries, sailors and prostitutes, drunkards and artists, adventurers and spies, all of them rubbing shoulders with the common man and the personal demons buried away within him. For Mac Orlan, this new ethos went hand in hand with the birth of the new century and the slow mobilization of Europe leading up to the Great War. "The social fantastic of our era," he wrote in *Le Décor sentimental*, "is the product of the great adventure that is industry. It is, in short, a new form of art, a new product of the human imagination that is going through its birth pangs."

While the social fantastic was hazily anchored in the contemporary, Mac Orlan still had a predilection for the old forms of his youth, and much in the same way that day conceals the night, the thrill of the adventure novel and the foreboding of Poe's visions have their place in Mac Orlan's work, hidden behind a thin gossamer curtain until the hours separating dusk from dawn. Conrad is very present, as are Stevenson and Kipling, but also Félicien Rops, the German romantics, Haarmann the Butcher of Hanover, Jack the Ripper, and Landru. And often surveying the scene from nearby is Mac Orlan's *pantin*, a woolen puppet of pale yellow with eyes like forget-me-nots, purchased in a small shop in

Wiesbaden. His golem-like companion, an embodiment of his superstition that was immortalized in a drawing by Laborde,[15] lived among the books in Mac Orlan's study in Saint-Cyr-sur-Morin. It also found its way into the more shadowy parts of novels such as *Malice* and *Mademoiselle Bambù*, and its echo is clearly heard among the "shadows with stretched chests" and "little mischievous legs [. . .] project[ed] onto the house at the corner of the street" in his 1924 poem *Simone de Montmartre*.[16] After nightfall, the *pantin* blended with the shadows and, alongside these many literary elements, melded seamlessly with the anxiety of Mac Orlan's social fantastic. As Raymond Queneau put it in his preface to Mac Orlan's collected works, "The social fantastic will be embodied by individuals who are nothing but, or are at least worth nothing more than, pig bladders or felt puppets—puppets who end up dissolving into the spongy, malefic fog or being strangled by their own shadows."[17] He continues:

> Although "literature doesn't always bring peace to the soul of he whom it nourishes," it does in any case permit him to examine his time and his contemporaries with a lucid and perfectly detached eye. He then, the writer that is, can give back to life the dignity that it loses in the bars of Rouen, Hamburg, or Tampico, or in the solitude of Foum Tataouine. He can then transform the smallest of lowlifes into myth, the vilest of actions into allegory, the most hideous of incidents into symbols, radiant and pure. While the active adventurer is busy with futile concerns like packing his suitcase, falsifying a passport, or taking a train at a given time—painful necessities for any soul given over to fantasy—the other pursues his intellectual adventure in perfect tranquility, carefully selecting the most figurative elements of his personal mythology: sailors and hobos, comrades on the Tour de France and gypsies, whores and pimps, mariners of fresh water or salt sea, pirates and gentlemen of the night, legionnaires of distant shores and men filled with joy. And they will haunt the privileged places of the Macorlanian geography, [. . .] a geography equally well-depicted by Brest, Le Havre, the canals of the north, Amsterdam, Hamburg, Altona, London, Chiaia, Galveston, Caracas, Tortuga Island, Sidi Bel Abbès . . . .[18]

Mac Orlan's work has been conspicuously absent from English translation. His Marcel Schwob–inspired tale of the sea *À bord de l'Étoile Matutine* was translated as *On Board the Morning Star* by Malcolm Cowley in 1924, and a few years later, Oscar Wilde's son Vyvyan Holland published *One Floor Up* (1932), a translation of Mac Orlan's 1930 crime novel, *La Tradition de minuit*. Fast-forward eighty-five years, and he has all but faded into obscurity. Even in France, his considerable output isn't often given its due, although many of his books are still in print at Gallimard. This has to do with a long-time shift in understanding: for many years now, it has become habit for us to relegate "genre fiction" to a subcategory of the novel, diversions for young people. While this has all too often been the case, it was not necessarily so when Mac Orlan and writers like him gravitated toward these genres in the first part of the twentieth century. Make no mistake: for the most part, Mac Orlan's writing is not pulp fiction. Yes, there is often an overlap in aesthetic with the classic dime store novels, with 1950s publishers like Gold Medal and Crest, to the point that much of the less nautically themed work can be considered "proto-noir"; but Mac Orlan's work speaks from a different time and a different mindset. Conceived by certain French writers in the early 1920s as a new mode of literary expression, the "adventure novel" of Mac Orlan's era had literary aspirations, and had not at all become the formula-heavy pulp industry that would later rise in the United States. As literary history attests, however, the latter mode would win out, and for many years the adventure novel floated along contentedly in a stream running parallel to but distinctly separate from the currents of "serious literature." Recent interest in moving beyond the stringent borders that sequester genre fiction from serious literature is not only opening doors to new writers, but can lead us to new appreciation for overlooked authors such as Mac Orlan, writers who may have fallen by the wayside as tastes shifted and trends were forged.

A poignant example of Mac Orlan's blending of the social fantastic with the adventure novel and a dark and latent surrealism, *Mademoiselle Bambù* is his particular take on the spy novel. In France, the Dreyfus Affair (1894–1899) had brought a touch of the fashionable to tales of espionage at the dawn of the new century, and while Mac Orlan was familiar with some of his predecessors in the genre, certainly Conrad and Kipling, possibly Chesterton, Buchan, or Childers, the French spy novel was late to arrive on the scene. There were earlier efforts in France, such as the *Naz-en-l'air* series by *Fantomas* creators Souvestre and Allain, but the first "typical" French spy novel is often considered to be Pierre Nord's *Double Crime sur la ligne Maginot* (Double crime on the Maginot line), first published in 1936. *Mademoiselle Bambù* predates it—or the first section does, anyway—by four years, although as the reader will discover, it hardly fits the mold of the classic spy novel.

Mademoiselle Bambù was written in several stages. The first section, *Filles d'amour et ports d'Europe*, originally stood alone, published in 1932 by Éditions de France. *Père Barbançon* appeared in 1948, and the two were slightly reworked and combined to form *Mademoiselle Bambù* nearly twenty years later in 1966. Deluxe versions of both titles were published in limited editions adorned with illustrations by Gus Bofa: *Filles et ports d'Europe* published by Au Moulin de Pen-Mur in 1946, and *Père Barbançon* via Éditions Arc-en-Ciel in 1948. These same illustrations are presented for your enjoyment in this current edition.

Chris Clarke
Summer 2017

ACKNOWLEDGMENTS

Special thanks to Renée Altergott, Heidi Denman, and Lara Vergnaud.

NOTES

1   Raymond Queneau, *Journaux 1914–1965* (Paris: Gallimard, 1996), 1006.

2   Pierre Mac Orlan, *A Handbook for the Perfect Adventurer*, trans. Napoleon Jeffries (Cambridge, MA: Wakefield Press, 2013).

3   Jean-Claude Lamy, *Mac Orlan: L'Aventurier immobile* (Paris: Albin Michel, 2002), 26.

4   Ibid., 52.

5   Ibid., 36.

6   Ibid., 34.

7   Ibid., 35–36.

8   As per French film historian Nino Frank, cited by Lamy, *Mac Orlan*, 84.

9   Guillaume Apollinaire, *Le Flaneur des deux rives* (Paris: Éditions de la Sirène, 1918).

10 The former were published by Jean Fort, a bookseller who kept shop in the tenth arrondissement (Lamy, *Mac Orlan*, 73).

11 Ibid., 72.

12 Ibid., 68.

13 Ibid., 70.

14 Mac Orlan, *La Lanterne sourde* (Paris: Gallimard, 1953), 25.

15 Argentine-born French engraver and illustrator of books by authors such as Francis Carco, Colette, Valéry Larbaud, as well as Mac Orlan titles such as *Le Nègre Léonard et Maitre Jean Mullin* (1920), *L'Inflation sentimentale* (1923), *Malice* (1924), and *Les Démons gardiens* (1937).

16 Mac Orlan, "Simone de Montmartre suivi de l'Inflation Sentimentale," *Nouvelle Revue Française* (1924). Translation published in *The Brooklyn Rail: InTranslation* (August 2012), http://intranslation.brooklynrail.org/french/simone-de-montmartre

17 Raymond Queneau, preface to Pierre Mac Orlan's *Œuvres complètes* (Paris: Cercle du bibliophile, 1969).

18 Ibid.

. . . *The words being these, (and the chorus so contrived, as most beautifully to mimic the peculiar laughter of* Toad-in-the-hole*):*

—*Et interrogatum est à Toad-in-the-hole: Ubi est ille reporter?*

—*Et responsum est cum cachinno: Non est inventus.*

CHORUS
—*Deinde iteratum est ab omnibus, cum cachinnatione undulante: Non est inventus.*

Thomas de Quincey,
On Murder as a Fine Art

GIRLS AND PORTS OF EUROPE

I

MEETINGS

And so it was in the grand lobby of a famous hotel on the Jungfernsteig, in view of the luxurious scenery afforded by the Alster, that I first became acquainted with the man whom I knew only by the somewhat imposing name of Captain Hartmann.

He was a well-heeled-looking man of perhaps some sixty-odd years. He wore a light gray suit made of that smooth, soft cloth that all men adore, an expensive suit, hard-wearing, a suit that must be set aside while still nearly new because of shifts in the fashion of the day noticeable only to men of a ripe age. Young people are always in fashion, or at least they give the impression of being so. And since life is naught but a series of impressions, it consists of marvels that appeal to us in vastly different ways than this one.

Captain Hartmann and I were made to meet one another. We drank some sort of pretentious concoction in the smoking room. We ran into each other in the hotel barbershop and then in the steakhouse. Captain Hartmann lived in a room neighboring my own, in the same corridor where elegant chambermaids surreptitiously peddled an array of erotic offerings of the finest quality.

Captain Hartmann was a Nordic whose true nationality I was never able to pin down. His clean-shaven face, the color of gingerbread, brought to mind the sort of faces we have grown accustomed to, like those of businessmen made famous by the advent of the photograph. He seemed to have been born of a German film and a slightly disturbing street song. To sum up, he unquestionably had the appearance of a wealthy man, that of a colonial soldier who had struck it rich; or, perhaps more simply that of an ex-convict who had found his fortune among the borderlands of a South American penal colony. We did not grow truly comfortable with each other until two weeks had gone by. Mutual acquaintances helped advance our relationship. After that, we were able to walk together, the two of us, through the fog and lights of the Reeperbahn. The Captain initiated me into Hamburg's nocturnal life, which is very beautiful, very mysterious, very dangerous, and, if you are one to possess an active imagination, utterly supernatural. We lived quite well, and, out of preference, at night. We loved the nighttime, which to us appeared to be the most acutely sincere décor of a Europe without direction, or, and this we dared not believe, more libertine than is allowed.

We frequented a mediocre little restaurant on the Schmuckstrasse: a small, rather traditional restaurant whose clientele appeared to belong to all of those social classes within which one might find clandestine human activity.

Captain Hartmann savored the night like a true connoisseur. He was inexhaustible on the subject, which, I will admit, did not displease me in the least. And it was with interest that I listened to his rhapsodic speeches about the era, the anxiety of the era, which was, according to him, an anxiety whose roots were nocturnal in origin. As we dined behind the restaurant's windows, which were hung with light curtains that gave the street the appearance of an aquarium, we could contemplate that working-class neighborhood where unemployment had left its mark.

It was no longer possible to make one's living by working; this seemed to be the end result brought on by the meticulously organized recklessness of modern society. Captain Hartmann nodded his head at each man who passed by, living illustrations of his long midnight allocutions.

One night, as it rained over Hamburg and unearthly clouds gathered together their aggressive horde out toward the sea, we went to eat and drink in Altona, alongside the Elbe, melancholy and as gray as lead. Gulls mewed along the water's surface. We were happy to warm ourselves as we looked upon that landscape of marine factories ringed by infernal brackish marshes not unlike those on the Baltic.

Captain Hartmann, having drunk a great deal, seemed bent on drinking still more. The wine acted on him, on his imagination and his memory, with a force that amazed me. It must be a question of race. The wine did not act gaily. It brought back memories as a sheepdog brings back its charges, each one of them in the prescribed order.

Night had come. The sky over Saint Pauli was lit in soft pink. Captain Hartmann, his hands in his pockets, legs stretched out, trunk burrowed deeply into an armchair, motioned before him with his hand, which held a lit cigar. He traced a word in the air that only he could read.

"The word is Lia . . . , L . . . i . . . a," he said in response to my gaze.

"Who was this Lia?" I asked.

"A pretty little thing. They also called her Mietze. She was a creature of the night whom I once knew and whom I lost, quite permanently, about a month ago."

"One more misfortune that can be blamed on the night."

"Do not speak ill of the night, or rather, do not speak too much ill of the night. You and I, we are ruled by her. There are two sorts of men: those who recuperate their strength as they sleep, and those who act. The night is rife with mysteries and revelations, or at least the night in certain cities I have known. Social romanticism, in each of its various forms, comes to her in search of that finery of the masses known as anxiety."

"Our society's raison d'être is to be anxious out of an excess of curiosity."

"Yes, anxiety is the shining light that projects the great films composing the public and secret lives of our time. The night indiscreetly reflects the secret thoughts of the daytime.

"In order to endure the night's dangerous charms, which are liberating for many, and for others allow for a basic state favorable to meditation, it is necessary to have confidence in the professions that allow us to make our living. Contemporary anxiety has two origins: it is of a moral nature that borders on the mystical among young people, and for men of my age, it is quite simply social. Some ask the gods for peace of body and mind, and others simply for their daily bread, as well as for the many trivialities of

domestic economics that this two-thousand-year-old cliché brings along with it. Well, that is where the danger becomes evident: men lose faith in their professions. The loftiest significance to be found in a profession, no matter what it may be, is to furnish security for our lives. Any profession that does not put food on the table is an element of revolt. Apathy in the face of misfortune is also an element of destruction.

"Take a look at Hamburg," continued Captain Hartmann, growing animated, "and tell me what you have been able to surmise. The daytime, which belongs to order, does not allow us to see the traces of social anxiety until the very moment it is too late to remedy them. But the night, be it in Saint Pauli, at the Alexanderplatz in Berlin, or at Place Clichy in Paris, the night is sympathetic to chaotic thought. It diffuses the images of despair projected by the differing fancies of each one of us. It is thanks to the night that social anxiety takes on the form of a strange malady of the individual and collective will. None of what I am going to tell you will serve as a panacea. All we can do is mutually provoke one another into becoming even more anxious, more sentimental, and, consequently, even further apart from one another. It is through the exasperation of our sentimentality that we forge enemies for ourselves. Sentimental people are, as with all those of old Europe, forever prepared to fight each other over details that are, at their very origins, exceedingly puerile. Hatred is born of a witticism or an inconsequential, misunderstood love song. Men will always fight one another over their love of the night, which is the true realm of individual personality and of the differences that can later take on the form of homicides.

"This evening, my dear friend, I speak to you in this way because my life seems no more moving to me than does my own reflection in the mirror. It is over, that is all there is to be said. And it comes to an end, more specifically, in an era that reserves no gentleness for the solitary misery of one's final hours."

The rain of Hamburg mutely accompanied Captain Hartmann's remarks. I had taken on a sponge-like demeanor, suitable to absorbing his words without warranting any complaint from this man who was so clearly beyond hope, yet who was also as curious to see and to hear as I was myself.

At certain times my past rose up in my throat and I was unable to spit it out. And so I understood the slightly solemn attitude of my provisory companion.

Captain Hartmann resumed his sermon:

"The dangers born of the end of the first millennium, that poorly described epoch, those traps are still set and at the ready within the old territories of social romanticism. The nights of the great cities of Europe, which belonged to the Sabbat the moment the ink was dry on the peace treaty, are still populated by enough stars that every man might hope to find the one meant for him. Not all of them are trembling in the sky. The melancholy of midnight gives the measure of the day. It is by roaming from street to street—in the way I do—and in those places where pleasures can be found, which, by definition, are public, that we catch sight of the true faces of those who are feeling the ground give way beneath their feet. We are romantic shades, you and I, well situated in time, and we understand that there is no gaiety there where gaiety only hangs by a thread. There is naught but the lights, which grow dimmer and dimmer still so as to better prepare the nocturnal spectators for the shadow's surprises."

Captain Hartmann called the waiter over for the check. We were brought our overcoats and we rode in a taxi toward the Saint Pauli quay, toward the small neighboring streets of the Marktplatz. The commotion of the festivities along the Reeperbahn allowed us to savor the dangerous silence over which the prostitutes kept watch, making their rounds up and down the sidewalk.

Hartmann and I smoked without exchanging a word. I let myself be guided, for the old man knew Hamburg well. There was nothing to do but learn from him as I allowed myself to be led about. And what's more, we understood each other too well for me to even begin to fear being disappointed.

"A month ago," said Hartmann, "I was once again wandering around near here. I ended up having a bit of an adventure, perhaps a sign of my senility, which I will tell you about later on, when the moment is right. For now, I am like a morally bankrupt man who opens his wallet before a friend to show him the stocks and bonds that were the cause of his ruin.

"This area disgusts me at the moment. If you don't mind, let us head back into the appetizing luxury of the Jungfernsteig. At this hour, the Binnenalster keeps vigil over the sleep of its legendary swans. The jazz will have concluded its frenzy; we will find some peace and quiet within the rich tranquility of a dreadfully opulent city. The night has come to an end.

"Everyone has uttered the cumbersome words of the night to the man or woman next to them. At dawn, isolation will come as it always does. A fresh isolation, bitter and slightly green. This is the way the whole world appears to us at first light, before the purchase of the first newspaper of the day, between the lines of which we hope to read of a genuinely new and prosperous occurrence."

Captain Hartmann sniggered. He raised his umbrella and hailed a taxi that was prowling nearby. He pushed me into the car.

II

CAPTAIN HARTMANN IS YOUNG ONCE AGAIN

"If you do not object," said Captain Hartmann, "I will take you along with me to a few of the ports of Europe where I have left behind certain memories. Recollections which, just a month ago, were once again taking shape in order to welcome me and rule over me. Thanks to a fortuitous gesture on the part of a handful of street worms, I managed to avoid having that ridiculous disaster impinge upon my dignity. Tonight, it is as a man liberated from the past that I wish to leisurely share them with you. You are a little younger than I, but you are reaching that defenseless age when the past takes its revenge and perpetrates irreparable asininities upon those who allow themselves to be governed by its misleading tendencies. Like me, I think, you must have known misery at an age when its disgrace is most fertile. Beware the honeyed rewards of misery and let its treacherous seductiveness fade into the pure and banal regret of your youth. While it might lack in originality, this manner of understanding your own past will perhaps save you from an aggressive recurrence of the violent, colorful misery whose meager poetic fire is kept alive from century to century by the many rogues and vamps of the street . . . At the very least since the days when the doors of literature were opened to the poor, to the wrongdoers and to the girls like those you will encounter in this short tale recounting a part of my life.

"When I arrived in Naples for the first time ever, it was roughly 1901 or 1902. In any case, the earthquake had not yet destroyed the city of

Messina. I tell you this because our stroll through Naples will inevitably lead us to Palermo, at the foot of Mount Pellegrino.

"And so, when I arrived in Naples, on the Piazza Garibaldi, it was night: a good night, thick, hardly a star in the sky, filled with Neapolitan mysteries. I might have been twenty-four years old. The exact number does not matter. The first modest-looking hotel I spotted on the Via Diomède Marvasi seemed adequate enough to shelter my temporary prosperity. A shabby bearded man carried my two suitcases. Madame Teresa's hotel was as mediocre as one could ask for. It would spare me premature concerns over the rate of a cold, impersonal room with high ceilings and walls done in sky-blue tempera, adorned by a patisserie-molded Pompeian frieze. A bed of iron, a bamboo washstand, a bulging, overly ornate chest of drawers, a filthy carpet, a filthy divan, a filthy armchair, and curtains heavy with dust gave the room both its character and its price. It was not expensive. It seemed pretty enough for me. Six weeks before my arrival in Naples, I had been rotting away in Rouen in a misery devoid of any romantic qualities whatsoever. I was working for a shipbroker. My departure for Naples had nevertheless been a logical move, but I will beg your forgiveness if I do not enter into detail as to why.

"It took me eight days to familiarize myself with the city. At the age I was then, we tend to explore far and wide. Naturally, a profound penchant for appearances led me to the Marina, along Strada Nuova or La Marinella. I would not have often been seen in Santa Lucia or along the Gradoni di Chiaia. Too many foreigners, in my opinion, detracted from the fragile picturesque qualities of that sun-drenched squalor. I have seen Naples again since those days. Its great commercial port is no longer the one I knew, not so much because of the logical transformation of its urbanity but rather from a singular but specious modification of its working-class values. Because of order, Italy has become a sorrowful peninsula, full of repressed instincts.

"In 1904, Naples was a beautiful city populated by a shameless throng wherein the children ruled. The scandals brought there by people from Northern Europe and North America dried in its sun the same way a hawker's marcasite treasures glint in the sun. Rumors of trouble surrounding the brothels and the naïve prostitutes entertained the very foreigners who gave rise to them. The balsamic air of the Gulf of Naples did nothing to calm the ardors of the senses, and if the naked youth who frolicked in the water before the Palace of Donn'Anna reminded one of the elegant perfection of the marble statues the law so staunchly protected, it is no less true that these same youth dallied far too often with the international esthetes who infected and ravaged the islands, from Ischia to Nisida, from Capri to Sorrento. God alone can understand just how much I grew to hate those magnificent demonstrations, dedicated to the 'Mother of Latin games and Greek delights.' I detest those whores to this very day—shut away in the garden of Greek roots, the Gerundive being passively declined from on high, the bourgeois of Pompeii and the Ablative absolute who knew Tiberius and the childish delights of his old age. In Naples, in those days, it was considered good form to both place the gods on pedestals and to whisper about them in the bedroom. It is true that those gods had seen others before them. They had all experienced unfaithfulness, which leaves one to wonder about the easy lives of the goddesses who overpopulated a sky that was without hygiene, without mystery, and without dignity.

"I likely don't need to tell you that I never spent any time on those islands, where they reveled in their own beauty during great celebrations since reimagined and reconstructed by queer librarians and lecherous antique dealers. There was singing in the trams that went out to Posillipo; they sang *Santa Lucia*, *Maria Mari* and that sort of thing. All the same, my memories of those songs are bitter ones, considering that those songs are worth more to me than any of that Latin drivel reconstructed under the seal of approval of Capri's beautiful skies, a sky made for esthetes with proud, dog-like nipples. If I had any love for Naples, in my own way, it was because of the rain that streamed along its leprous walls, turning the gutters into small rivers. Then, the brazen youths who paraded their virility before the foreigners would hide themselves in darkened doorways, eating oranges or polenta. Their eyes gleamed in the shadows: they were actually luminous. I had made the acquaintance, along the Marina, of a few Bersaglieri in red chechias—their light uniform—who belonged to an international battalion. They were at times garrisoned in Naples, at others in Tripolitania or

Eritrea. They were big, solid Piedmontese fellows, the sort who could be counted on and who they called *forestieri* in Naples. Quite frankly, they did not speak the local language, and so that designation is appropriate. We would get together to drink wine: the sort of wine that didn't require poets to sing its praises, wine that was merry and easy to drink. A girl lived among us, of mixed race; she was nearly white but she stood out next to the Neapolitan women, who were short and thickset. Quickly enough, prostitution brought ugliness to those who lived the life. The tavern was also frequented by lowlifes, but they sat at a different table. They were dressed according to the fashions of the day, in light-colored three-piece suits, but garments so dirty, so sullied by stains that it was impossible to believe in the sincerity of their wearer's stylishness. That misery went well enough with violent death. And yet, violent death itself wore a jester's mask.

"Now, the girl I'm going to tell you about was known as Signorina Bambù. In Palermo, she was called Miss Annah, and in Hamburg, Mietze, or quite simply Mam'zelle Bambù. During the Great War, she was ordered shot to death on a parade ground, in Nantes, I believe. Nothing is known about her execution. Matters of espionage have left few traces. Mademoiselle Bambù was a spy, devoted to her profession; of that there is no question. I did not know this when I met her in Naples along the Corso Garibaldi. By that point, she was already entertaining the soldiers until nine o'clock at night and the officers until daybreak. In the afternoon, she received civilians and then spent time putting her observations in order. The most boisterous of the rose-crowned profligates who enlivened the Saturnalia in Capri was named Hugo Breyer. He was a fellow countryman of mine of whom I am in no way proud, plucked straight out of the sort of Greek poetry you find in every anthology of erotica. Basically, I think that this Hugo Breyer was involved in these sorts of diversions in order to give himself a particular mien. He hoped to compromise himself with his choice of lifestyle so as to be left alone in his other pursuits. It was he who directed this mixed-race beauty's covert activities during the whole of that period. For Mietze, who was half Cuban and half German, well, Hugo Breyer's lifestyle made her stomach turn, as they say. For those sorts of liberated women have odd aversions which for them serve as morals. A corporal in the Bersaglieri who happened to be from Milan introduced me to Mietze, which is to say to Signorina Bambù. Straight away I was taken with her, for this was a woman who made her way through life spreading the same sort of sentimental ambience that was my own. Signorina Bambù spoke German frighteningly well. My choice of the word 'frighteningly' is appropriate, for to hear that golden-brown mélange speak the language of Goethe without the slightest flaw could be considered an occurrence of the fantastic that was particular to Europe, one that we are still enduring today.

"In the evening, after dinner, our footsteps rang out on the sidewalks. Signorina Bambù was vivacious, cheerful, and in no way a vampire. She looked rather like a young schoolteacher of color who had been entrusted with what they call a 'special mission.'

"As for me, I was surprised that they had the first bit of curiosity with regard to the activities of the Italian army. That appears to have since changed. But in that era, Italy thought very little about its soldiers and, other than a few battalions of Bersaglieri and the navy, the rest of the mobilized youth and those who commanded them had grown more and more disinterested in a war that no one could then imagine.

"Signorina Bambù took care of me. She would take my head in her hands and say to me, 'Repeat this, repeat that . . . I love you, you love me, we love each other.' She would conjugate the verb *to love* for me in Italian as if she were force-feeding a chicken. I laughed like the young man I was and I wholeheartedly caressed my Hamburgerin of Cuban origin.

"She had danced at . . . She was familiar with the sailors and their somewhat overrated exoticism. In Naples, she spent her time with commercial seamen and officers of the British Navy over from Malta, red-faced, obese men. I lived among the wisps of shadow cast by her secret life. I followed her as my shadow followed me, and I knew nothing about her other than all the secrets of her supple body, smooth and hard like well-polished, tan wood. When she was naked, she glowed; her body illuminated my bedroom, from where I could hear the trains whistling northward. Naples could become saturated with tender sorrow in the same way a sponge becomes saturated with water, and Naples was overwhelming to me with its inordinately sunny charms. Signorina Bambù, guardian of the shadows, allowed me to fight against all of the agile lies brought into being by the sun and fortified by the heat. The Neapolitan filth stuck to my hands. Twenty times I was on the verge of leaving, of tearing asunder, with an adroit gesture, all of those classic images of May evenings in the streets of Chiaia or the Borgo Santa Lucia. Signorina Bambù put a finger to her lips and said to me, 'Wait!'

"I loved that woman as only a young, fairly sentimental man is able. I flittered along behind her, all the while boasting when she was not around. And of course, I repeat, I in no way suspected her clandestine activity. I believed her to be a girl who practiced prostitution very intelligently. As such, she belonged to a sort of purely literary aristocracy. At the end of the day, Signorina Bambù was, for me, a literary creation. I loved her as one would love a schooner, an ocean liner, a locomotive, a hunting rifle, a well-designed cabaret, a stretch of houses, an unknown city seen at dawn from the exit of a deserted train station.

"One day Signorina Bambù invited me for tea at the villa of Mr. Hugo Breyer, near the Via Amedeo. It was at this time that a complicated-enough character took shape inside of me who would end up being what we now designate by the name Captain Hartmann. Captain Hartmann is not a man but an accumulation, a group of individuals, a series of events . . .

"'You will come to Palermo with me,' Mademoiselle Bambù said to me. 'You will be my secretary . . . Isn't that right, Mister Hugo Breyer?'

"To which Signorina Bambù added, 'If, of course, that suits you.'"

III

PALERMO AND SIGNORINA BAMBÙ

"The train that was carrying me from Messina to Palermo chugged along through a forest of bergamots whose heady and cheap perfume made its way in through the compartment's open windows. I was not traveling with Signorina Bambù, but instead in third class with some artillerymen from Villa San Johanna, soldiers who wore dark blue tunics, their leather belts painted lemon yellow. Such was the uniform of the Italian artillery in the years before the War of 1914. The four or five soldiers were from down near Syracuse. Their manner of speaking in no way brought to mind the Latomia. They were thin and loud. North Africa and Greece had leaned over their cradles like two good fairies: the first bestowing upon them the art of speaking very quickly while waving their hands in the air and the other entrusting them with the principles of a republicanism that was underhanded but for the most part without violence. They were complaining about the government, and they didn't know the first thing about the operation of the cannons. And when I say 'cannons,' that is exactly what I mean, for we are talking here about a field howitzer that was still rather rudimentary. Even before it was put to use, this cannon was famous for the ingenuity of its brakes. I do not suspect that Signorina Bambù or Mr. Hugo Breyer believed for a second that my involvement in this business would be of even superficial use to them. I had never been able to take seriously the role played by military spies. The ones I knew had always given me the impression of being rather juvenile. The sort to direct a battering ram at an open door. They were like those illustrious philosophers who disguise fundamental truths

beneath a vocabulary of their own invention, one that is quite naturally incomprehensible. I was too young to take my role seriously, yet conversant enough with human folly to make a tragedy of it. Signorina Bambù appealed to me for intimate reasons that were far enough removed from that reputed-to-be exact science we call espionage. I loved that woman with her light-brown skin; I followed her as she moved from place to place, and, as she was rich enough to provide for my needs, I felt an enormous sense of satisfaction in having fallen for a young woman who was able to cover the costs of our emotional and carnal partnership.

"To make a long story short, there I was in Palermo without having been able to extract any information from our artillerymen other than a few bawdy songs of which, I might add, they had not managed to remember all the verses.

"Palermo, in my opinion, can no longer even be considered a European port. This charming city, spread out at the foot of Mount Pellegrino on the ocean side and, further inland, at the foot of Monreale, was not very animated circa 1904. The port itself contained a few small fishing boats, some sailboats tasked with fostering trade relations with Tunis, and a few freighters that were grimy but of a visibly greater importance. As I awaited the arrival of Signorina Bambù, I stayed at a small hotel near the Quattro-Canti, amidst the very heart of Palermitani life, which was not exactly exhilarating. I didn't feel the need for exhilaration, and since I was in love with my foreign-born spy, the thought of roaming the streets in hopes of meeting girls hardly crossed my mind. These girls were terribly impressed by the Chasseurs à Cheval garrisoned nearby, and the sailors of the English Royal Navy, come from Malta on their gray-painted destroyers. That lot seemed like serious clientele.

"The Mediterranean air, the very lifeblood of Palermo, is subtle and mild like the air that gives an oasis its relaxing qualities. My arrival in Palermo coincided with the entry of an ocean liner into the port, which put its passengers ashore for the day. There were English among them, and among those English, Mr. Hugo Breyer, done up like a cavalryman: riding breeches, a well-tailored Norfolk jacket. He was sporting a cap that made him look younger. His face, this time without glasses, seemed more likeable to me.

The smallest detail can be all it takes to make someone seem more likeable. He walked up to me without any signs of familiarity or friendship. I had already grown accustomed to the protocols of espionage. I did not show any surprise when Hugo Breyer approached me and politely asked, in a loud, clear voice, the way to the Questura. No sooner had he finished, he informed me, in a hushed tone: 'Tonight, at seven o'clock, in front of Santa Maria della Catena.'

"With a tip of his hat, he moved on in the direction of a waiting carriage whose driver was motioning to him invitingly.

"I had a few hours to wait. It dawned on me during those slow-moving hours, which I spent in Monreale looking at the mosaics, that the political lives of my new friend and my lover actually concerned me. I made my way back down from Monreale on foot without availing myself of the tram, in the company of a few chattering peasant-women, *contadina* who were carrying fruit to the city. I found them pretty, but at the same time rather timid and mistrustful. One young girl with beautiful, gentle eyes was a delight to look at. She was looking at me as well, and kept turning back toward me. She was full of sweet, naïve curiosity. For that very reason, her mother was also turning back; she intercepted one of my smiles and slapped her daughter, who followed her off whining and complaining. She was just a little girl, about fifteen years of age, but she seemed to mandate strict surveillance by her mother.

"By well before seven o'clock, I was lurking about in front of the church. I was deeply preoccupied. My wallet, however, contained five hundred-mark bills and a thousand lire. I could cut and run, if need be, leaving Hugo Breyer to conduct his political activities alone. Alas, Signorina Bambù stood part way between the screen where the film was playing out and my eyes, which were no longer those of an ordinary spectator.

"At precisely seven o'clock, I spotted the Signorina coming toward me. She gently greeted me, quite openly and without any semblance of secrecy. I kissed the tips of her fingers.

"'Sweetheart,' she said to me, 'you have nothing to worry about with me. You need to understand that there is no way in the world I would ever intentionally put you in a difficult situation. If we have need of you tonight,

Hugo Breyer and I, it is only because the service you can provide us will in no way endanger you.'

"'I'm not worried about a thing, Mietze,' I replied.

"'Of course not, of course not. Then follow me . . . We are to meet Hugo at the Greek Gate.'

"On the way there, Signorina Bambù stopped three or four times to kiss me, full on the lips. The occasional passerby turned to look away, smiling indulgently. In Palermo, a relatively quick kiss, in the middle of the street, was not going to stop traffic. At least it was like that in those days.

"At the Porta dei Greci, Hugo Breyer was waiting in a taxicab. It was only then that I noticed my companions' outfits. Signorina Bambù was dressed very shabbily, which was quite unlike her. As for Hugo Breyer, he looked like a loutish sports enthusiast, the sort you saw often enough in those days near the velodromes, especially around the time of the six-day races like the ones held at Madison Square Garden in New York.

"'Get in, and whatever you do, keep quiet,' said Hugo.

"I hesitated a bit, and, coming to a decision that I recognized as rather hasty, I parked myself on the car's jumpseat. The Signorina's full, round knees slipped in gently between my own. Hugo Breyer wasn't all that bad when he made an effort to act like a commoner. His cold and glabrous face would have served as a good model for the youngsters who had surrounded us yesterday in the Schmuckstrasse 'Lokal.' The automobile, which let out an irritating screech as it went, carried us toward the Kalsa, the working-class area that stretches out at the foot of Mount Pellegrino. We came to a halt across from the entrance to a narrow alley. It was more or less night. Very near to us, a cavalry trumpet sounded out a melancholy call or farewell. The evening trumpet calls of all the world's cavalries are even more melancholy than the song of the swan, which I have only ever heard played on a violin.

"'What a job,' opined Hugo as he stepped down from the automobile.

"His jacket climbed up slightly at the back and I caught sight of the butt of a Colt sticking out of his hip pocket.

"My own pocket was also bloated by a similar weapon. I have always owned a revolver; out of pretension at first—as was the case in those days—

and then out of necessity ever since. Six weeks ago, I still had a very nice Browning. I don't have it any longer; it was taken from me. But a man my age doesn't really have any need for a Browning. Youth alone can participate in the aesthetic that firearms always end up imposing upon those who serve them. For it is never the man who wields the Browning, but instead the Browning that wields the man.

"The car was dismissed and we remained there, the three of us, at the corner of an alley that ran along a large wall in a state of disrepair. Hugo Breyer pushed us into the shadows cast by the wall.

"'You will remain here,' Hugo instructed me. 'Nobody will come, unless it's a car, a Mercedes. It will stop here, in front of that vacant house across from us.'

"'But there's a light.'

"'Nein . . . it's one of ours.'

"'The car will be driven by Karl. You will introduce yourself. You will tell him, "Everything is fine, they are occupied, and I have been instructed to tell you to wait for them."'

"'For how long?'

"'As long as it takes. All night, perhaps.'

"'Aren't you worried that the car . . . that's to say, a car, here . . . at this hour.'

"'Nein, nein. Here, a door down from this vacant house, girls entertain their clients, foreign visitors . . . Put out your cigarette. You mustn't smoke . . . Stay in the shadows and keep watch for the automobile. See you soon.'

"Hugo Breyer steered Signorina Bambù before him. They were soon lost to sight as they carefully followed the shadow cast by that tall wall, illuminated in blue as it was by the Moon, the lovely blue of shadow cast upon snow.

"Once I was alone, the first thought that came into my head was of flight, or, more specifically, the desire to carefully and quietly make my way toward the port, then on to my hotel, and from there one hop at a time from the train station to Messina, the ferry, an Adriatic port, and Austria. It wasn't as simple as all that, despite the fact that I had five hundred marks and a thousand lire in the inside pocket of my Norfolk jacket. The love that

I felt for Mlle Bambù was not yet so strong that its radiance could dissipate the ill thoughts of that clear and fragrant night. In the distance I could hear the rumble of the sea. Having your back to a wall behind which something is afoot can, after an hour, bring about unpleasant turmoil within a man's reasoning.

"Without thinking, I began to urinate against the wall, my mind a thousand miles away, as the saying goes. My ears pricked up like those of a fox at dusk, I attempted to make out, coming from the direction of Palermo, the typical sound of a large automobile, louder than the cars that creep up behind us these days. I gazed at the illuminated window of the vacant house: a five-story house, the tallest in the Kalsa. An enigmatic house, arbitrarily cleared out for some secret reason. Three hundred feet farther down, the cathouse seemed lifeless. I would have given anything to hear the ordinary clink of glasses, the uproarious brouhaha and an occasional touch of profanity. The house was silent. All of a sudden I felt as if Mount Pellegrino was about to come crashing down on me. I took a few steps into the shadows and I spotted the stationary Mercedes, its lights extinguished, Karl (perhaps) at the wheel, and, in the back, four men, three of whom wore the classic hat of the Carabinieri. And so . . . I ran nimbly, along the wall, in the direction taken by my companion and Hugo Breyer. I came across them as they too were scampering along beneath the wall.

"'There's a . . .' I said, out of breath, '. . . a Mercedes, parked at the corner. It's full of Carabinieri.'

"At that, Hugo Breyer and the signorina turned on their heels. Mlle Bambù hiked up her skirts and ran hard, her knees high. To see that woman running as fast as she could filled me with an abominable fear. Yet we flew, all three of us, our elbows in tight. At an intersection of the alleys, Signorina Bambù gasped, up close to my face, 'You go right.' I dashed, alone this time, down a narrow alley littered with jagged stones, between two rows of cacti and agave."

IV

MARSEILLE AND THE CAPTAIN

"Here, I feel obliged to omit a few details," said Captain Hartmann. "It seems necessary to me, because one must never capitulate to the proclivity for unabridged public confession. The propensity for unexpurgated public confession, which is as shameless as it is desperate, is evidently driven by a substantial compulsion. It remains to be seen just how much we will feel the exigency to surrender to this substantial compulsion. Our propensity for war is not a product of public confession. But is war any less revolting than a murderous peace?

"Although I was associated with an organization of spies, and one of them, Signorina Bambù, was prettier than you can possibly imagine, I felt no hatred for the police. I fled before the police, but I admired them. Ever since that enigmatic night when I had been forced to take flight, running like a cloven-hooved satyr amidst the exacerbated odors of the Latomia of Syracuse, I have never been able to prevent myself from feeling some affinity, perhaps unhealthy, but tremendously fervent, for the police, their secretive side, their mythos and their ceremony. It is impossible to imagine anything more aesthetically pleasing than a police car packed full of Schupos, brandishing silence and powerful searchlights able to probe the thickest shadows. In Marseille, at the Fort Saint-Jean, I was waiting somewhat anxiously with a meal of rather unattractive rations in front of me even though I had already decided to withdraw myself from the world for the next five years. I was dreaming, my eyes open, of the future of Europe, of war, and of the police. My Palermitani adventure had led me to imagine the war, or more precisely its monstrous and deceitful preliminaries. In my mind, war and the police were joining forces in order to create a new state. I was mistaken, quite naturally. To this very day, this subject of meditation costs me many painful hours I cannot seem to avoid, even with the assistance of those remedies which help by offering one a sound sleep.

"The consequence of war is to force people to reflect carefully on the fragility of human life, especially those who lack imagination. This is a type of meditation that is rich in images. It perpetuates a fertile melancholy, and those who fall prey to it never go long without experiencing the effects of the violent reactions that stem from these same melancholy meditations.

"War is a fact, the reality of which is quite banal. It is a more or less aesthetic reduction of nature's own rhythm. But destruction, when its constituent parts are made up of humanity—and this thanks to the excess tragedy of which it is comprised—becomes a boundless source of cerebral creations which move back and forth between the two moral forces of humanity: hope and despair. It is nearly impossible to provide any sort of explanation in the face of a violent event that provokes fear among some and, with equal power, self-sacrifice among others. What we are able to control with more certainty is precisely those arbitrary creations of thought, which, on occasion, take on a puerile symbolism. Blood is a social value, although it is less esteemed than gold. We are quicker to sacrifice our blood than we are gold, because the sacrifice is spontaneous, and because gold is often the material fruit of a lifetime worth of struggle. But blood is rich in imaginary pageantry. It is at the origin of the deepest mysteries, those which demoralize the crowd and trip up our reason. Around spilled human blood there roams a strange cortege of ghosts, the description of which is interminable. Human blood spilled by way of murder starts all of the brass wires of the telephone and telegraph humming. The murderer, despite his wishes, feels the entire weight of the world on his shoulders. For blood is a poetic social value, and poetry is a form of indescribable torment for those who cannot elevate their souls above certain common desires.

"Accordingly, in every era that follows a great war, the thought of bloodshed brings about unpredictable reactions. These responses become the essential elements of romanticism, to which we could give a clearer, more accurate name: the social fantastic.

"This fantastic assumes different appearances in accordance with each era, but the popular anxiety is nevertheless the same. The practical applications of science only reinforce this fantastic imagery, blending it with new mystery. The more dazzling the light, the thicker the shadow. It is always in the shadows that humankind likes to seek out its anxieties; the shadows of the best-lit cities provide food for the strangest worms."

Captain Hartmann lit a cigar, and blowing the smoke far out in front of his face, continued his tale.

"If the Earth has by now been discovered, if the crossing of the Sahara or the Gobi desert is no longer any more than a sporting exploit from which we hope to gain little in the way of revelation as the better part of it is already known, man and his moral domain still conceal all the secrets of adventure. Faced with certain acts, faced with certain crimes—it would be easy to provide recent examples—the imagination of man remains confounded. It is possible to anticipate the picturesque outcome of a voyage to the Far East, but it is impossible to predict the sometimes terrifying expression of the secret inner thoughts of a man, woman, or youth. This loathsome mystery tempts the public curiosity and lends a certain appeal to any tale describing such a criminal act. The horror of these tales is contagious.

"This is the reason that, at least for the classic creators of this fantastic, men who often deeply shake the sensibilities of a nation, policemen often land at the top of the list. Around them gravitate all of society's most worrisome individuals, a single one of whom can shatter the social harmony that has been valiantly defended by this great multitude of brave men. An assassination always gives rise to a great number of exegetes, which demonstrates to which point it stimulates the curiosity of the public. Defending against wrongdoers in no way prevents the somber curiosity their actions give rise to in the crowd.

"War among soldiers is frank. For that reason, it is almost straightforward. But the wars conducted by spies, being of another sort altogether, force us to pass through into this secret domain of the human race, and afford a magical-seeming liveliness to the most familiar landscape and the everyday encounter.

"And so the police have become the most working-class expression not only of the crowd's taste for punishment, but also of its penchant for the many manifestations of the social fantastic that adorn small, often peaceful towns with elements of the unknown. The number of novels devoted to the police is so great, in all honesty, that it unequivocally reveals the immutable power of the shadows, which is to say the fear of murder, more terrible than the fear of death. As in all things, the trappings and the picturesque aesthetic they carry with them surpass the importance of their constituent parts. Death drives adventure only so far as it knows how to ride on the novelistic coattails of the social fantastic.

"The policeman towers like a beacon above the unwashed masses of the wrongdoers, above the informants who, morally, are hardly any better, and above the spies—but like a beacon whose light remains dim until surging forth at the moment of the guilty party's arrest. Before that supreme shock, a supernatural fog envelops his silhouette. Silence dampens his footsteps. He is everywhere, like a guardian wraith, relentless. Without seeing anything, we can sense that he is on the hunt. The streets, woods, and fields are all subject to his will. He is, quite honestly, a peculiar figure who casts a radiance upon the real, bestowing it with a life that is thoroughly indescribable.

"His personality is made up of a thousand personalities, and each one of them cultivates its own specialty. He is strong, because the indignation of the people animates him. He possesses the terrifying willpower of the sophisticated automaton, because unlike the evildoer, he is without passions. I can readily imagine the modern policeman to be like one of those bizarre laboratory humanoids whose physical appearance is lacking the details that afford the human shape its seductiveness.

"He is a steel-jointed machine with a mathematical sensitivity. Electricity runs through a network made up of a multitude of wires ending at his brain. He is not unlike the camera, for which the true face of things, hidden behind appearances, is developed in double exposure as it is with film. He works out his own deductions via a series of waves meticulously recorded by an invisible receiver. This figure, who must be armed with every possible mechanical means in order to see and hear, quite naturally takes up position at all the worst street corners, where sinister thoughts whirl round like dead leaves.

"The police officer, equipped with antennae and lights capable of revealing the most remote sounds, can thus attain the limits of a poetics of policing. It is in this moment that he enters into the literary, into that category of literature fed by contemporary visions and which, of course, has nothing whatsoever in common with the many popular novels where the policeman and the brain trust of a police force play a role that has today fallen into obsolescence.

"I hope you will excuse me for this outburst of police-themed poetry once you are aware that I was a part of said institution up until the year 1919. At that time, I became wealthy in a manner that was as uncontestable as it was banal: an inheritance. I tendered my resignation and I regret it to this day. I could not have done otherwise.

"That interruption of my life lasted five years. Starting point: Marseille, 1903, and back again: Marseille, 1908. That period of nullity made me into a lean man, both physically and morally. All of my fat melted away in meditation, first near Colomb-Béchar, and then later Oujda.

"When I returned to Marseille in 1908, I was attired in the navy blue pea jacket and similar-colored pants worn by the French colonial infantry. But, and remember this detail, on my head I wore the red kepi with the blue turban, embroidered with an inverted flaming grenade. By this mark, I was recognized as a legionnaire on liberal leave, back from Tonkin, or Tuyen-Quang to be more precise. For the rest of my life, I will carry with me the impression of maternal tenderness that Marseille offered up to me as a gift when our second-rate cargo freighter, which had nearly broken up before reaching port, abashedly presented itself before one of the most famous cityscapes in the world. Marseille sparkled with beatitude on the shores of a sea as blue as those featured on tourism posters. You can always rely on them to give you a middle-of-the-road perspective of a group voyage. I was

traveling in a group, since I was in the company of thirty-five soldiers, haggard and lean from bouts of the ague, from kicking the gong around, and from imbibing too much of the local 'choum-choum.'

"Yes, it is possible to miss Marseille without any senile weeping, as it is a welcoming city, equal parts philosopher and girl next door. Its extraordinary slums, at that time beyond compare, glowed in the light cast by nonchalant friendship. As soon as I was permitted to break with my military past, I went off in the direction of the Old Port, to see a man named Loriani who had a pub and a small restaurant where they served shellfish and *pieds paquets*. I had given his address to my regiment, saying that he was a cousin of mine and would set me up with civilian employment. Loriani had served in the Legion. Since those days, he had lived in Marseille, his wife running the bar and he taking care of his various side ventures. That was the side of the ledger I was interested in ending up on. There, as quickly as possible, I hoped to find enough to make ends meet, to add a little butter to the spinach, as the French say. I found my man Loriani in his canteen on Rue Bouterie. It was already famous. But you wouldn't come across any shifty Neapolitans there, nor any overexcited Arabs. You would only see a knife pulled for the right reasons, and no one would raise a finger against anyone who in turn intended no harm. The 'cageoles,' vamps as brash as they were unsightly, wouldn't steal your hat in order to lure you down an alley to get your throat cut. Artists frequented the neighborhood. They were well received. They ate and drank in the brothels' private dining rooms. They were asked for counsel and never for money. All of that has changed quite a bit, much as everything has, veering in the direction of malignity, toward the profoundly malign, studied as one studies for a profession, malignity without enthusiasm, treated the same as you would an office job.

"Loriani, jacketless in a pink shirt, an imitation Panama hat on his head, greeted me at the door of his restaurant, which he had decorated with an unambiguous sign reading *Au rendez-vous des primards*. Since then, this restaurant has become known as *Au rendez-vous des Matafs*, borrowing from the sailor's *argot* of Toulon. There is drinking, there is anything you could want. It's the same old story. Nothing changes less than vice, except

for perhaps stupidity. Loriani wiped his salt-and-pepper mustache and wrapped his arms around me.

"'Well, old friend, you will eat well with us. Come in, I have so many things to tell you.'

"He introduced me to his wife, a good Marseillaise woman, a little petulant but prodigiously well spoken. Oh sure, 'business' was great! Her cooking was good and I was pleased to get reacquainted with Old Europe by landing directly in front of a skillfully made and well-balanced bouillabaisse. In those days, I still put up with the prejudices, and I don't mean of good cuisine, but of that famous cuisine considered to be an art form. What a ghastly affectation! In their hearts, all men have the desire for a simple meal: a steak, French fries. As for the rest . . . The stomach's memory soon enough forgets.

"Loriani housed me at his place for the next two weeks without asking me for a thing. But it was not as if I was penniless. I had known how to get by in Tuyen-Quang as well as any crooked sergeant major from the French Marine Infantry. I had returned with five one-thousand franc notes, enough to live off for a year if I behaved sensibly. I was not concerned about this in the slightest, as I did not drink.

"With Loriani's persistent and detailed recommendation, I was introduced to Mr. Galfin of the municipal police, who straightaway suggested I make my way to Paris, where I was to find the director of the judiciary police, to whom he wished to recommend me. I returned to Loriani's place feeling rather satisfied. In my pocket, I carried a letter of introduction which would gain me entrance into the same terrifying power that had forced me into frantic flight for the five years and two months that led up to that conclusion. Gribouille's strategy, which consisted of throwing oneself into the water when one fears it will rain, had never seemed ridiculous to me. I have always followed this principle as best I can, each time that it has been possible to do so.

"Is it the blue of the Mediterranean waters, that elegant sailboat pulling into the Old Port? Is it that Neapolitan song, 'A Canzone Mia,' heard one evening on the terrace of a little café on the Quai Rive-Neuve? Whatever it was, the voice of a beautiful young street singer always works its way down to the very depths of my soul. A depth of five years—that is really something. A vision of Signorina Bambù rose up halfway between my eyes and the songstress, who was just a sixteen-year-old kid decked out in a two-bit blouse and a skirt with holes in it. All the same, that young girl was proud of her station. As she sang, she sashayed back and forth past the terrace where I was enjoying a Pernod. A fairly skillful guitarist was accompanying her. People were tossing her pennies. I threw her some francs. She saw them, gathered them up, and approached me, still singing *Maria Mari*, swaying along like that other one, the one from the Via Marina in Naples. Although younger, she resembled that unforgettable mistress whom I had not seen since the perilous night in the Kalsa.

"The guitarist dragged the girl farther down, toward another terrace. The memory of Signorina Bambù, whom I called Mademoiselle, was alive there on that sidewalk, before my eyes. This younger version was taking her place. She belonged to the same species of humanity. Her father was black, her mother white, the mischief twinkled in her eyes. I called out to her, but the man with the guitar said to me, 'Let her be, you understand? She's not for you, Madame is married.'

"Mlle Bambù number two disappeared into the former red-light district. I had to swallow my emotion. How old would the real one be now? Perhaps thirty. She had been no more than twenty-five when I used to hold her, sitting on my knees, in the open-air *baleras* of Santa Lucia and Torre Annunziata. I had thought I would be able to see her again without any of that intense disappointment that so definitively kills the past. At thirty, a girl as lithe as Bambù would have held on to her beauty, the seductiveness of the professional dancer. The manifestation of this young Neapolitan girl amounted to nothing more than a paltry degradation of the image of a woman whom I tried to age five years, using every trick of the imagination. This sort of prudence has protected me my whole life against the many sentimental deceptions that make up the future. The thought of death had never interfered with my memories, even when, more or less despairing and disillusioned, I was moping around on my bunk back in Viénot. I had managed to flee and, with the feeling that they were hot on my trail, I had enlisted in order to find a starting point stripped bare of my past. But I had read the papers. My adventure in Palermo seemed to have left no trace whatsoever. If I never heard anyone mention Mlle Bambù again, at least I would never have a reason to imagine that she was dead. Hugo Breyer never faded from my memories, either. The vitality of that man had won me over, and for a while thereafter, I had often caught myself imitating his bearing. It was rather infantile. One day, as we pursued a target among the Beni Snassen, in an area which was already part of the French conquest of Morocco, rumor had it that a German adventurer, or some said a German cavalry captain, was leading the Riffians who had come down from the Spanish Jebels. The first thing that entered my mind was that the man might be called Hugo Breyer. I pictured him in sirwal pants and draped in a brown djellaba; I recognized his thin, hard face under the tightly wrapped turban. Of course, I had never been able to rein in my excessive imagination. One night when I was asleep on my feet alongside the men of my company, it seemed to me that Signorina Bambù had joined our dusty troop. She carried my Lebel for me, and smilingly accompanied me without a word. We were kicking up more dust than a flock of sheep, but she walked on without it bothering her, with the walk of someone who is doing a good deed."

V

PÈRE BARBANÇON

"I'm about to let you in on an observation that I often relied upon during my career in the service of the Special Missions. Espionage is a bit like any other game of chance: you have to hedge your bets if you hope to break even. For this reason, I was in the service of Germany, England, and France at the same time. I used my skills to obtain certain merchandise that was without value insofar as its authenticity was not guaranteed. Taking the needs of each of them into consideration, I sold this merchandise to the highest bidder. It was necessary to extract any value I could out of whatever hogwash I came across. It wasn't always easy. Espionage calls for a considerable literary capacity, and the section heads are not the supermen some people would have you think. They are individuals who think logically; by simply understanding their logic, you can feed them little gifts from which they in turn can try to profit. First and foremost, spies are entrusted with the job of spying on each other, setting traps for each other, stealing secrets from each other, and providing a hint of the mysterious to the idle gossip of easy women, a mystery that is often turned tragic by circumstance. For the most part, spies do not believe in the actual value of their merchandise. They themselves are quite surprised to benefit from information which, to them, seems anodyne and often improbable. Spies, and especially female spies, are quite ingenuous, and often talented little coquettes. Those of that ilk never understand the first thing about the trial at which they have been sentenced to death, and when facing the gallows or the firing squad, they consider themselves the lamentable victims of a dreadful judicial error.

"To return to my own case, I served my apprenticeship with a private police agency whose headquarters were located not far east of Paris. A curious business, that agency. The chief was an Armenian. I can no longer recall his name. He lied like an old woman and never wanted to pay us. One evening, when I no longer had a red cent left with which to have dinner and pay for my room, I emphatically demanded the two hundred and fifty francs he owed me. I was exasperated by a tail I had been sent on in the March rain. Since nine o'clock in the morning, I had been following a young provincial whose parents were having him kept under surveillance for reasons which had in no way been shared with me. He was a half-wit, but that was not the problem. That blockhead kept me running after him for eight straight hours; he was inexhaustible . . . unless he was simply enjoying leading me all over Hell's half acre. Well, I headed back to Le Raincy, wetter than a waterlogged sponge. I demanded my due. My boss sidestepped the question. And so I gave him a proper beating. He scarcely tried to defend himself and held out a pair of hundred franc notes.

"There was no longer any question about staying on with the police, unpaid and without capital. It was then that I decided to cross the Rubicon. After a series of maneuvers, the recounting of which would be quite tedious, I was given a recommendation to meet a certain No 28, who worked in the service of the Germans. It was impossible to determine the man's origin, in my opinion, much as was the case with my own. The other numbers and I referred to him as Père Barbançon.

"It was in Brest, in the heyday of the neighborhood known as Recouvrance, two years before the war, that I first met Père Barbançon. I joined him at a table in the Café de la Marine, which, in those days, was enjoying an evident period of prosperity. There you would find the 'little allies,' girls later made famous in print, as well as midshipmen, students from the *Borda*, and tasseled hats taller than that of the legendary Angiboust, whose name you have surely heard in passing. Père Barbançon appeared to be polite and well known by all. He seemed to be quite at home in that noisy and joyous *brasserie*. All the young men of the navy would get together there. The subdued uniforms of the lieutenants of the colonial infantry, in from the barracks that had been erected in front of the old prison, would mix with the sober uniforms of the marines. Not as many red trousers. Père Barbançon, apprised of my visit by agent No 7 in Paris, was waiting for me with a *choucroute garnie* on the table in front of him. He was a large man in his forties, unkempt and pot-bellied: a red face and a redder beard cut quite short in the Florentine style. As far as anyone knew, he ran a ship chandlery at the merchant port on the Quai de la Douane. Oh, that shop! The perfect backdrop for a film by Pabst! More than anything, it was the back room that was worthy of admiration. It was furnished with a round table, a canary cage, six chairs, and the presidential armchair occupied by Père Barbançon. In one corner, stood up like an ornamental suit of Japanese armor, gleamed a full diving apparatus in all its coppery glory. The kitchen, which sometimes served as a darkroom for the development of the occasional snapshot, opened directly onto that room. One could leave through the kitchen and find oneself in a back alley that led to Rue du Chemin-de-Fer. Père Barbançon's shop thus had two entrances, a rather pointless safeguard seeing as everyone was aware of both of them.

"But let us return to my reception. Père Barbançon greeted me with a smile, his hand casually held out. 'My dear friend, it's so good to see you again.' He had never seen me before. But that cordiality created an instant bond between us by eliminating the sentimental small talk from the unknown that made each one of us seem enigmatic to the other. It felt, with very little effort on my part, as if I had known Père Barbançon for a long, long time.

"I offered him a glass of lager and then, quite amiably, we left the Café de la Marine and made our way to the shop on the Quai de la Douane, which was as I have just described it to you.

"Père Barbançon removed the door handle from the door and offered me a seat in the back room. He settled himself in the armchair. 'Number 7,' he told me, 'had additional instructions for you. They were delivered to me by a traveling salesman who distributes nautical tunics. You are considered an intelligent man, well enough educated and courageous; this last term was attributed to you after an inquiry made with the second foreign regiment with whom you served. Here, then, is the social situation which is to be made available to you, and which will permit you to work away from prying eyes. For starters, I am to hand this wallet over to you; it contains all the identification papers necessary for you to legally assume the name of Joris Gouma, a native of Hindeloopen in Friesland. You are to inform yourself about that small Dutch port. Your occupation is that of a long-haul captain, your license is with the other papers. I suggest you spend some time studying the art of navigation so as to not say anything foolish at the Café de la Marine or elsewhere. To all appearances, you will take command of the *Medemblick*, whose first mate is a consummate sailor, which ought to set your mind at ease. Mr. Fischer belongs to our group. But his role must remain that of the true captain of the *Medemblick*, which will afford you the peace required to do your work. The *Medemblick*'s mission is to purchase and raise up wreckages in hopes of turning some sort of a profit from them. You will need to study up on this subject. Here are several pamphlets I have selected for you, accompanied by written notes which will give you the appropriate tone for an ordinary captain who wishes to go unnoticed.'

"That was the day I was given the title of Captain. The following day I took possession of my cabin, and the *Medemblick* weighed anchor to go ascertain the resting place of a small cargo ship foundered off the Isle of Quemenes. During that operation, which had me away from Brest for three weeks, I had the time to rather artfully adopt the personality of a Dutch sea captain, business-minded and responsible. For this was not simply a matter of me hitting the bars with the hat-wearing gals at the Café de la Marine and those without hats over in Recouvrance.

"My mission, which I can tell you about now that all is over and done with and has been for quite some time—at least I hope so—consisted of searching for sites that would allow a submarine to put ashore a few men so they could pick up some supplies and, on occasion, establish caches of petrol in those places. Regarding these activities, I wrote long, detailed and precise 'commentaries' which I then handed over to Père Barbançon, who then forwarded them to God knows whom.

"I am not a spiteful man, I am not a great patriot, and I am not full of hatred . . . but that occupation, which did not seem dangerous to me, was well-suited to my fondness for instability, mystery, and easily made money. I must remind you once again that everything I was doing seemed juvenile to me. I couldn't quite convince myself that one day, in the not-too-distant future, Germany would profit from my information.

"You know the story of the submarine that torpedoed the convoys off the shore of Brigneau-en-Moëlan. The German officers who were in command of it had on many occasions gone ashore for a bite to eat, wearing their oilskins. They spoke proper French, and my goodness, in an oilskin, a German naval officer is not all that different from a naval officer from France or England.

"I quite liked Brest, which in those days was a first-rate military city. That poor town has undergone quite the transformation since then; I saw it again after the Great One, worn to the bone by war and especially by the new treaties linking your countries. The picturesque charm of that beautiful city at the farthest end of Europe was melting away before our very eyes.

"For me, having known it in 1912, 1913, and 1914, it had become unrecognizable. It made me experience a feeling of bitterness that was soon joined by the suddenly awoken memory of my lovely half-Cuban, Signorina Bambù. The Rue de Siam rolled out its spectacle, the women's costumes filling the tourists with wonder. All of that has disappeared. The medieval girls from Plougastel, those from the very strict Pays de Léon, and the downcast of Ushant all now wear modern sweaters. Thankfully the headwear has persisted, accentuating the gentleness of their faces. There I knew an island girl . . . What is the use? *But that's all shove be'ind me, long ago an' fur away. An' there ain't no buses runnin' from the Strand to Mandalay.* Remember the song?

"I remained in Brest until the beginning of July 1914. Then I grew afraid, a lucid fear that would make me sit bolt upright in my sweat-soaked bed sheets. I saw the future before me. A sky of warning dictated my conduct.

"Père Barbançon, still smiling, was now careful to look behind himself when he went out. Evenings, he double-locked himself in his shambles of a room. This behavior was visible only to me, but it did not encourage me to persist in my profession.

"Without saying a word to Père Barbançon, whom my departure must have plunged into even deeper anxiety, I left for Rotterdam, already having an age-old idea in my head. Thanks to my hardy constitution, I was induct-ed into the Legeer, which is the Dutch Foreign Legion. After six months on base, sporting the black shako embellished with orange stripes, I boarded a ship and we set sail for the colonies.

"It was on the island of Sumatra, in the tropical brush of the Batak peoples, near Lake Toba, that I was wounded in the shoulder, stabbed by a poorly poisoned dagger. My head had been the prize at stake in that match played out next to a jammed machine gun.

"This all took place while, at Verdun, you were once again defending the route to Paris."

VI

THE CAPTAIN SEES HIS OWN BLOOD

"In 1918, upon the signature of the peace treaty, I was eking out a living in Berlin as the manager of a nightclub in Neue Nönigstrasse; a small, second-rate cabaret frequented by scrawny working girls and freshly demobilized hoodlums. I was not happy there among those people. Nevertheless, my duties as manager of a fairly dubious 'Lokal' allowed me, once again, to enter into a relationship with the German police. In times of trouble, policemen grow even fatter. They are able to eat and prosper without a care in the world, because a regime change, which can be murderous for some, changes nothing for them other than the design of their uniforms. Sometimes it just so happens that the turmoil is far-reaching enough to warrant a completely different uniform. That was the case. As for me, I wore no uniform. During a revolutionary period, one can advance quite quickly within that extensive organization housed at the headquarters on the Grunerstrasse. Two or three cases that earned me praise gave my immediate superiors the idea of sending me abroad to work in collaboration with New Scotland Yard, along the bank of the Thames.

"At Scotland Yard I encountered some charming folks, admittedly quite military in their bearing, but perfectly courteous and refined. After all, the English race as a whole is refined. That alone should afford them some sympathy. The men of Berlin, my employers, were less refined than the English, and as a result less likeable than the English. Thus caution with our words became necessary when it was a question of the administration of 'public affairs,' for no gaffe would be forgiven us. The same does not hold

true for the English, who could bungle things at their leisure thanks to their being refined.

"I lived in London for two years following the war. I speak the language comfortably, with a touch of an accent, like a 'Dutcher.' I was accredited in the eyes of the English police, who were helping me with my search for a particularly vile criminal.

"I love London; London is my second home. It is a city that abounds in those elements belonging to a society built on appearances, one which I continually discover as I move about from one day to the next.

"What else can I say about London? I don't know where to begin. I lived near the port because of my search. I know the ports better than I do Mayfair. Which was not where I was invited out to dine . . . My hunting grounds began at Scotland Yard and ended in the west toward Barking. That place is an old Elizabethan memory, one which still serves me as a reference point.

"The Tower of London and the yeomen key-totes, those 'Beefeaters' draped in scarlet and gold, watched over the city on one side and to the other, the countless docks. From Westminster, outmoded bells that are typically lost in the fog answer one another and mingle their carillons with the long grinding of the trams that trace their way along the Victoria Embankment at top speed.

"From the Saint Katharine Docks all the way to Beckton, the two banks of the Thames are cut up much like a chessboard, each square a pier occupied by freighters, lifts, hangars, cranes, and audacious gangways. The boilermakers' hammers accompany the monotonous clickety-click of the winches. The trucks smell of pepper, rum, and anything else that might be acquired from beyond the Suez to help one forge a thoughtful temperament such as my own.

"Wapping to the south and Shadwell to the east demarcate London's famous docks, whose black, calm waters reflect nothing less than a landscape of human activity dedicated to the glory of that amazing grocery store that is the high seas. This age-old scene, which has remained seductive thanks to the enigmatic occupations of the men who resided there, has since been lost. Even the knaves invented by Sir Anthony Trollope have long since relinquished their place in the minds of children. Obviously, it takes a very vibrant imagination to perceive the constituent parts of the social fantastic as it exists among the more dangerous classes, which is in a way the starting point for all worthwhile adventure novels. In Wapping, near the tunnel stairs, used to lie the Execution Dock, which was a topic of conversation on every sea and was witness to Captain Kidd's last dance. Humankind has not run out of curiosity with regard to these sorts of places. If memory serves me, it was in 1701 that the public hanging of Captain Kidd took place, in front of an average-sized crowd and a few sturdy seamen who knew whaling songs better than they knew the Bible, not to mention the paths that lead from one tavern to the next, all the way around the world.

"From Wapping, one can see the seventy hectares of water that make up the Surrey Commercial Docks, over where they lie on the other side of the Thames. The rails trace arabesques of mercury on the ground, the piles of lumber break up the view, and South American freighters unload frozen meat as if it were a souvenir of the war. I often took that ride in a Scotland Yard car, for the monster I was looking for was most likely employed, according to the extensively examined probabilities, in that flat but strangely mobile vicinity. It was a menial search that demanded patience, for as you head down toward Barking, the docks are lined up one after the other. I was crossing the West India Docks, which are devoted to rum. They are reached via Commercial Road and East India Docks Road, two well-lit thoroughfares, where my shadow alone preceded or followed me at night. Finally arriving at Poplar and Limehouse, at the Chinese quarter you may be familiar with, which is more or less London's version of the Chinese Barrio.

"It is enjoyable, for a policeman who, as a part of his profession, must keep his imagination stimulated, to wander as night begins to fall upon those two uncurving streets lined with little brick villas, comfortable-looking, but each one of them containing tragic, shifty, and perfectly silent elements. Posters painted with Chinese characters are pasted over some of the windows of those run-down cottages, aiming to attract the yellow-skinned sailors who often occupy the stokeholds of the cargo ships. There is rice inside those mournful and filthy 'clubs,' there are women, and there is also opium. My colleagues at New Scotland Yard are relentless in their pursuit of these Chinese, the opium merchants. They hit them often enough that they can just leave them where they are. The drug suppliers live in the area. They put on airs of being honest businessmen, but even so, of unsettling businessmen, often with white women in tow, miserable creatures dazed by alcohol. As soon as night falls, at roughly the hour when the traffic on the neighborhood's roads comes to a stop, the Chinese roam in groups, with muted steps. You do not hear them coming. They pass from one sidewalk to another, and disappear like ghosts. They go first to one person's place, then another's, to play games, squatting down in a circle on the floor. They pay no mind at all when the door is opened. But when, on a whim, it entered my head to open the door of one of those dwellings, I caught a glimpse, in the half-light, of an extraordinarily pale girl, of broken mugs on makeshift shelving, questionable linens heaped up in the corner, game players, and children, whose look of misfortune exceeded any real-world expectations.

"The ladies of Pennyfields were saturated with alcohol, to such an extent that from afar, their state of stupefaction took on an angelic appearance. They looked like the fallen angels of the night. Their actions seemed to be dominated by the absurd ideas brought on by alcohol. All of that led to a certain dexterity in their thievery. Those doleful sirens watched the drunken sailors carefully, from the lowliest coal-trimmer to the captain in his bowler. These girls and the Chinese, their partners in crime, made up the two decorative features of Poplar some ten or fifteen years ago.

"Also in Poplar, not that long ago—I believe the establishment still exists—was a curious dance club run by a Mr. Charlie Brown, famous for his ivory collection. When I knew him, Mr. Charlie Brown was a fat little man with a mustache and a triple chin. He wore pants, to be sure, but these were pants with exceedingly short legs and immense bottoms: clown pants. He was quite intelligent, and he knew some stories that were not lacking in charm. His establishment sold beer. It was consumed by people standing up in a space that looked like the back room of a junk store. There is little need for me to admit to you that I spent the odd night at Charlie Brown's place, down among the docks of the port and among those who made a living on

those docks. He knew my profession. I remember those nights well. Surrounded by perpetually drunk girls dressed in ways you could not even imagine, girls who danced as if they were mechanical dolls. The men gallantly supported them, the type of men you always find in those sorts of establishments, by which I mean confidence men, bumbling stooges, and some very good people. I can tell you that Charlie Brown's bar reminded me somewhat of the Lapin Agile, or the Lapin à Gill, if you'd rather, the one in Montmartre, the way it was about ten years before the war. Charlie Brown's regulars came from farther afield. They came from the sort of people who go from London to Colombo in the hopes of finding a hot meal.

"The people of the night who hang around in Poplar can also be found, as you surely know, in Hamburg, in Antwerp, and in the large ports of northern Europe. The foggy landscape lends them a certain literary distinctiveness. The daytime disperses all of those ghosts. For in truth, they are nothing but ghosts who for a time follow their fate beneath the great electric lamps of Commercial Road. Other men than I—Stevenson for example—have come across these ghosts on the beaches of Oceanian islands, which give me the impression of being fairly welcoming places. They are also to be found in the margins of the old police annals. Their rather limited set of traditions, as colorful as they are cutthroat, remain constant regardless of the change in setting. In the port of London, from the rooster's first crow, or more precisely from the moment the first boilermaker's hammer strikes its resounding note on a sheet of metal, the ghosts slip back into their own individual mysteries. Some of them blend into the anonymous crowd of dockworkers, others, rucksacks over their shoulders, return to their ships. As for the girls, they sleep, perchance to dream the dreams that give appeal to their lives.

"Yes, the great docks of the port of London absorb this film under the broad light of the day. Nothing remains of the images of the night.

"Weary of dragging my feet along the deserted sidewalks, I was returning home, empty-handed and discouraged as I witnessed the break of day over the Thames. It was like the triumphant song of an immeasurable city where commerce takes on an appearance that is as solemn as it is poetic, if you consider poetry to be the artificial embellishment of unavowed sentiment. In my mind's eye, I can still see the first scene of the day as it unfolds in the vapors of the Thames by way of a young and weak pink sun. The navy firemen extinguish the last fires from atop their lively, scarlet pump engines. A sluggish, unburdened freighter commands the river. It is heading for the sea, toward the seven seas, that extension of the London docks, to wherever the compass rose will take it, a Rose of the Winds decorated at its tips by a piece of the British flag. Ah, my dear, patient listener, how melancholy it is for me to play out this documentary film.

"Thus it was that one night in Poplar, the past abruptly showed up and placed itself directly in my path. A little before ten o'clock that evening I had stepped out of a public house where I had the habit of drinking a pint and eating a good, rare piece of meat with a few potatoes. It was not far from the Whitechapel police station, where I was to meet Sergeant Fyster, one of my friends from the organization. It was raining. I was in a hurry, the collar of my overcoat turned up, when I experienced the professional sensation that I was being followed. I turned around and sure enough, farther down the street on the same sidewalk, I spotted the tall, bulky shape of my pursuer. I could not make out his face, as he too, because of the rain, had turned up the collar of his overcoat, more specifically an appreciably rumpled beige gabardine raincoat. I came to a stop, and the man crossed the street. He then stopped in turn, tying one of his shoelaces. He promptly turned away, and without hesitation I made my way toward him while he also retraced his steps. Having reached a narrow alley, he entered. I went down the middle of the road so as to also reach that alleyway. The fellow's behavior was making me nervous. Pulling even with the alleyway, I came to a stop, trying my best to scan the shadows of the doorways from a safe distance. I didn't see anything, which led me to take a few steps, approaching the mouth of that dead end which seemed to me to be rather suspect. My hand instinctively clutched at the butt of my Browning in the pocket of my overcoat. I was not to make use of it. A small burst of flame tore through the night. I could tell that I had been struck in the shoulder as I could not get my loaded pistol from my pocket. Two more blasts rang out. I had to press myself against the iron shutter of a shop and then, all of a sudden, I made out the massive yet strangely nimble figure of Père Barbançon. He was fleeing down the sidewalk like a rat.

"Three revolver shots in the night, in the streets of London, is totally unheard of. Policemen came running from every direction, then a group of Cockneys, two or three women, some unemployed, two soldiers from the Irish Guards.

"I could vaguely hear the muddled sound of the onlookers' voices as they discussed the attack. And then I felt myself sliding down a hazy but irresistible crevasse towards the very center of the Earth.

"The result, good sir, two bullets: one in the shoulder, and another fortunately blocked by a rib. There is no need for me to say that Père Barbançon was not found. Nor did I do anything to assist the law. That ancient history from Brest could hardly help my relationship with the English police. I relinquished my tongue to the cat, and as I healed I promised myself that as soon as I was able, I would forsake the port of London, because I had been recognized, and, for that reason, my cover had been irrevocably blown. I knew Père Barbançon well enough to convince myself that, after that first show of force, he would not be content to let sleeping dogs lie."

VII

MEMORIES OF SIGNORINA BAMBÙ

"I was in the service of the British when I left for Barcelona, once I had re-covered from my injuries. The Intelligence Service, which is quite a lovely institution, and about as unsentimental as you might imagine, thought to make use of me provisionally. In that celebrated institute of curiosity, the term 'provisionally' is a watchword. It is impossible to say that a man has committed himself for the rest of his days simply because he comes in con-tact with one of the game's anonymous pawns. You remain a part of the company as long as those in charge of the company have need of your ser-vices. It might last a week or it might last twenty years. The man who put me in touch with x of the Intelligence Service was a young writer who fre-quented a rather dingy club where, each evening, in a very stripped-down setting, there were discussions about the future utility of man, who was considered to be a basic machine that was less perfected than he believed himself to be. Before getting to be the hero of a more colorful mission, I was forced to suffer through a number of these speeches and drink tea with young artists of both sexes who knew Montparnasse well, and who were completely at odds as to what they liked about it. How those charming young women with their come-hither eyes wasted their time in that dull club. Anyway, that is none of my concern. One thing led to another, and always by the same methods, always in the presence of the same people— who were more enigmatic than they were intelligent—I was supplied a passport for Spain, which, in those days, not all that long ago, still bore the likeness of a king. I was to pay a visit to several Spanish ports, to get to know

those on the inside, and more specifically, to take charge of furnishing deto-
nating caps to the Riffians by means which were not completely devoid of
romanticism. My sole function consisted of delivering the munitions. I was
not expected to drag them across the Moroccan Rif, nor to get them across
the border into French Morocco. That concern belonged to some men
from Tettauen and Tangier, which is an open city in name only.

"It was morning when I entered Barcelona. The urban landscape
which offered itself up to me the moment I stepped out of the train station
triggered no emotion within me. It was beyond that neighborhood that the
true Barcelona, the one whose literary splendor tormented me, would reveal itself. I remained calm, for I knew I would not be disappointed. A taxi
brought me to my hotel in the Calle de San Pablo, a small hotel that was
both tranquil and discreet. Its operator, a Luxembourger woman, wel-
comed me amiably. She must have been well informed on a good many
subjects, but she was never indiscreet. Later on, I discovered that she belonged to the brotherhood. She had knowledge of certain details about
Mata Hari and the manner in which she was arrested. The proprietress of
that hotel was called Mme Lordeau.

"It was quite naturally in the Chinese Barrio, which is in the process of
disappearing, that I took my first steps in that city. I was ineluctably driven
to spend the day there, and then the night, not with the intention of carous-
ing in the nightclubs targeting the dockworkers or foreigners, but in the
hopes of interacting with a blue-collar, revolutionary element whose en-
deavors could be of interest to me.

"There were two aspects of the Chinese Barrio that seemed to have
been melded into a single misery yet which differed from one another entirely. The brazen gypsy women, who smiled for the prurient satisfaction of
the passing trade, could not compare to the poor women who labored re-
signedly in order to raise entire cavalcades of children whom the climate
protected in spite of everything. The poverty in that area of town was ap-
palling. In the Cuartel del Atarazanas, the neighborhood that lay behind
the artillery barracks, there wasn't much to live for, just shameful scraps.
They were dressed in rags. The happiest women were once again the prostitutes. And there is no reason for me to exaggerate. Some evenings, ten

women would shamelessly eye the heel of a bottle left behind by a customer, whether out of considerateness or satiation. They would rain curses on each other when it came to making off with a glass that was still full. I never once saw them eat; most of them survived on alcohol alone. And all of this only a short distance from the Rambla de Santa Mònica, which in the hours around daybreak has on many occasions offered up the sight of a man pirouetting at the touch of a bullet or two-stepping with the blade of a knife. Political crimes, naturally. For me, the Chinese Barrio was pretty much the perfect picture of a southern European hell. So that I could breathe, I would go and sit in a wicker armchair along the Ramblas, and there I would watch life as it was paraded before me, breathing in the scent of the canna and listening to the canaries sing. What beautiful young women! I marveled to see them go by in joyous groups, arm in arm like the brave little workers they were. They authoritatively rebuffed the young admirers who were trying to impress them. This brought a laugh to the young soldiers in their berets and khaki uniforms, numerous as they are in Barcelona and in particular along the Ramblas and the Paralelo, which is to the Reeperbahn what the Spree is to the Seine.

"This man, the respectable merchant to whom I was providing the cartridge primers, Joan Labet was his name. He lived in the Carrer del Cid Campeador and operated a soda business. He owned fifty or so small cars which he rented to poor bastards from the area, who went on their way about the city selling their sodas, along the Paralelo, on the Ramblas, from the square at Plaça de Catalunya all the way to the one that lay before Portal de la Paz. Naturally this low-paying venture, which barely brought in enough to let the renters of the little cars get by, was nothing more than 'window dressing,' as they say, meant to conceal another more important and lucrative business.

"Joan Labet was wealthy. He owned land outside of Ceuta, and rental properties in Ceuta itself, the lot of it in his wife's name, a jealous and devoted woman. As for her jealousy, she was able to enjoy it in solitude, for Joan Labet often left her to her own devices. Incidentally, it is quite rare for a young Spanish wife to follow her husband around everywhere he goes. This ridiculous male attitude is really only suited to shopkeepers in their

Sunday best. In any case, each to his own. I was not living in Barcelona to busy myself with the mores of the working class or those of the bourgeoisie. The matter I had undertaken was not without its own dangers, and sometimes, as I bathed, I would wistfully gaze upon the two scars I bore as a reminder of Père Barbançon.

"As far as my own business went, I spent the morning in my small office in the Barceloneta area, in the Calle de Alegrina. I was only a few steps away from lunch at Soler, where I reveled in langoustines with fresh tomato. As far as everyone else was concerned, I was an orange exporter. I had worked it out with a broker from Valencia and my true profession was well hidden from sight.

"My nights were spent pleasantly in the Chinese Barrio. I was sleeping with a little dancer from the Paralelo. She was innocent, and above all she was healthy in body and mind, which made her priceless. They called her La Chulapona, and I have never understood why, as she was relatively calm. She was a dark-haired, golden-skinned kid, a slight young girl from Sants, born in the neighborhood behind the prison. In some ways her countenance reminded me of Signorina Bambù, who had added flavor to my life in the days when, by virtue of my romanticism, my life was still susceptible to being flavored.

"La Chulapona danced until midnight. Afterward, she would throw on her drab little coat, don a tired-looking cloche, and come to find me in a very discreet café in the Calle Mediodia, near where it meets Calle del Arco del Teatro. That fairly peaceful bar was never watched by the vice police. A few gloomy, loquacious revolutionaries ate there, ham that was nearly black with pan-fried rice. My associate Joan Labet received his refreshment sellers there, settling his accounts with them at a table in the corner. After which we played cards and discussed the fate of the Spanish king, who seemed to me to be in a great deal of trouble.

"Joan Labet knew the secret life of Barcelona well. He had been involved with espionage during the war, on the part of the Germans. In those days, Barcelona could have been considered the international spy fair. They rubbed shoulders on the Ramblas, staring at each other, appraising one another's worth right down to the nearest penny. There you could find Ger-

mans, English, Austrians, Belgians, Turks, Swiss, Italians, French, and Por-
tuguese, all of whom were moved only by one idea: purchasing the right
document and reselling it for a profit to whomever it concerned. All of the
cafés along the Ramblas were chock-a-block with spies, to the point that
they had almost become decorative. There were many women for whom
the intentions of the higher-up officers of the navy were not the least bit
secretive. Or at least so they would lead you to believe. The number of easy
women who were shot by firing squads is actually quite considerable. The
majority of them still believed, the night before their execution, that all of
the fuss was nothing more than a good laugh, to put it mildly. They would
collapse with a look of astonishment on their faces. But not all of them
were of that sort. Some of them knew how the game was played, its ups and
its downs. These women were aware, one way or another, of the two poles
of their fate. They were cunning, courageous, cruel, and more devilish than
the men. Quite naturally, all of those social qualities were concealed within
a seductive body and behind a seductive face. Joan Labet had dined with
most of those ladies. And that is how he came to speak to me very quietly
one evening, one on one, about Signorina Bambù, who was still referred to
as Mademoiselle.

"The tale he told played out like a film, the sentimental charms of
which would cause suffering to only a few, myself among them. During the
war, Mlle Bambù had been living in a charming old apartment near Plaça
Reial. Cadets from the Escaudra, the barracks of which was not far from
her abode, would stroll past her windows. It wasn't possible to imagine anything more 'old Catalonia.' Bambù was passing for a rich Cuban. She threw
parties, entertained military attachés from the four corners of the globe,
and, of course, spies of both genders by the bucketful. That young woman
was still working for the Germans. Her loyalty surprised me. Joan Labet did
not attend her gatherings. The more ornamental role he had taken on led
him to spend his time at humbler soirées: those of the street and the Chinese Barrio. But through intermediaries, he was kept abreast of the beautiful half-Cuban's actions. Thus he knew that she still worked for the same
employer. Once in a while, Signorina Bambù would turn up on the Paralelo,
without suspending her role-playing. She was followed by a host of suitors

who all outwardly had the look of idlers, but who were in truth far too occupied. She had no desire for their attentions. Mata Hari's example illuminated the night of the solitary female spy. Many grew sick of the profession at about that time. Signorina Bambù was in no way one of them. One beautiful summer morning, Joan Labet noticed that all of the shutters of Signorina Bambù's apartment (she was known as Mrs. Anita Wood in Barcelona) were shut. Which was ordinary at that time of the day . . . the housekeeper would take care of it. Joan Labet returned that afternoon. He spotted the cook talking at length with two or three of the other good women of the neighborhood. They went into a fruit seller's shop. Joan Labet followed them in and asked for some oranges. While he was making his selection, he overheard what he wanted to know. Madame had not returned home for the past three days. Madame had left with three men, a closed-top automobile waiting for them in front of her door. She had not been seen since, nor had she left any instructions . . . All of which suggested a murder. A month went by. The time had more than come to face facts. Mrs. Anita Wood, or more precisely Signorina Bambù, had been lured into some sort of rat trap. It could no longer be any question of a sudden departure, nor of flight. The first hypothesis could be verified. Thus Joan Labet learned what he wanted to know, which is to say that our beautiful friend was in France, in the sightlines on a firing range in the southwest. Apparently she was shot and accorded the military honors then in use. When word reached Barcelona, it was necessary to keep any sincere anguish to oneself. This was not agent No so-and-so who was to be missed, but rather a nice young woman who would often go by on the Ramblas around eleven o'clock, her arms laden with flowers, followed by her bulldog Pums. An unknown fellow, who didn't seem the least bit concerned about compromising himself, had a mass performed in the Church of Nustra Señora de Belén. He sobbed solitarily into his handkerchief before the surprised looks of several other spies, who then placed him under observation. It turned out he was just an amateur, a delicate man who had little to do with the war, a man whom circumstances had rendered immoral and with whom I must disagree. For one must admit that the unfortunate Bambù reaped what she had sown. She was definitely a part of the war. It was her trade.

"While it is admittedly lacking in detail, you will understand if this account of the final adventures of Mlle Bambù plunged me into the deepest despair. My grief was literary. I sought out all of the books that dealt with the public, romantic, or secret lives of female spies, without discriminating as to which side they were on. A special sort of lechery kept me in suspense, an erotic fetishism that dominated me and compelled me to search out carnal pleasure in the arms of a spy, or in those of any woman who seemed to me to be of a similar nature. Fortunately for me, that madness did not last long. I regretted my own past too much, now that I had grown older, to become a slave to the past of a woman.

"The memory of Signorina Bambù melted quite naturally into my own recollections. Still today, it haunts me; it surfaces, but does not exceed the limits of its role in my reflections on that subject. To be clear, I should say that three weeks ago this memory was still mingled with my own. Since that date, I have made peace with myself and no longer have any regrets.

"As for the business with the detonation caps for Abd el-Krim's cartridges, it ultimately didn't cause me too much trouble. I was under the protection of a few generals in the Spanish army who, by betting on both sides, were most certainly acting to the detriment of their own men. It was at that time that I fell in with Kleim, who had been a legionnaire like me. He is now in prison. A peculiar adventurer, with a dark sort of energy. They say he was sold out by a woman. Perhaps. You will always be sold out by a woman if you have any commercial value. Myself, I have no commercial value, in spite of my wealth, which is in any case quite recent. I am wealthy, but I am still simply known as Captain Hartmann."

VIII

REFLECTIONS, RUE DE LA SAVONNERIE

"You are familiar with Rouen and its admirable oil port that eats away, a little more each day, at the verdant prairies bordering the Seine. Mme Deshoulière's sheep have long since been turned into gigots. I speak of this without enthusiasm because I am not fond of mutton. For that very reason, I would take a can of gas over a gigot d'agneau. And so I would do nothing—even if I could—to prevent the green countryside that lies between the transporter bridge and La Bouille from conceding a little terrain each day, yielding great fertile swaths of its realm to the water, which would trace yet one more basin. Rouen's oil docks make for a large and handsome port, constructed as if to taunt the past that lies at the heart of this medieval city, jealous of both its ancient form and its Nordic origins. France is a Latin nation only in order to give itself a style that appeals to it, of course. I have lived in Rouen several times over the course of my life. The first time was a long time ago, some months before getting to know the unfortunate Signorina Bambù in Naples. She who was 'cut down to size,' as you might hear it described in Place Pigalle, by the rifles of a service squad. I lived in Rouen, exchanging labor for a room in the home of a draper in the Rue des Carmes with the hopes of learning business and French. I was a regular at the Théâtre des Arts and I took it quite seriously, like everyone else, when there was a premiere. The port of Rouen, since that time, has taken a giant leap beyond simply being charming countryside. In a few years, it will join up with Le Havre and Paris. Separating Paris from Rouen, along the banks of the Seine, will be nothing but wharves loaded with the many classic trappings that go along with them.

"The high-freeboard freighters, emptied of their merchandise, towered over 'Petite Provence,' where I was warming myself contentedly on the terrace of a café. I was picturing Joan of Arc in that setting. She would ride by, crossing the Corneille bridge on horseback, one hand on her thigh, followed by an artillery trumpet, chubby-cheeked and sardonic. A film about Rouen, shot at any point between the past and the future, ought not to overlook these details. Not too long ago, I was sent to Rouen, after a more than honorable reinstatement within the ranks of the police. I still had a good many friends inside that great building neighboring the Alexanderplatz. I was entrusted with a mission that reminded me of the one I had been given in London a few years earlier. You surely know the elaborate story of the Düsseldorf crimes. The outcome we are all aware of has by now diminished the public interest, and more importantly the mystery. At that time, we knew nothing about the personality of that maniac. He was often compared to Haarmann the 'Butcher' of Hanover and Jack the Ripper. On the basis of a denunciation that might have seemed intriguing, I was sent to scour the streets of Rouen, those that lead to the river port by way of Rue de la Savonnerie. I presented myself as an accordionist. A man carrying an accordion in his arms, as long as he knows how to make use of it, has very little to fear and can go pretty much anywhere. I had learned how to play the accordion for my own enjoyment. I acquired the perfect instrument, a marvelous Italian model that gleamed under the street lamps like a treasure described in fairground poetry. My box in my hand, I was properly attired and freshly shaven with a white scarf tied around my neck, a gray fedora on my head at the correct angle. I followed the Rue des Charrettes without incident. At the corner by the Théâtre des Arts, I hesitated. Should I head straight toward the quays or turn down Rue de la Savonnerie? A dance club, the lights out at that hour, indicated the road I was to follow. I thought I heard voices. They spoke the working-class slang of Berliners. But it turned out to just be an occupational hallucination. That is how I happened to inadvertently walk past the Océanic Bar. The owner stood in front of the door: the legendary Canadian. He was an exceptionally powerful man whose face brought to mind that of Mr. Edouard Herriot. The 'Canadian' was taking in the street air in front of his bar, tied to that section of sidewalk. He spotted me and called me over. We drank a glass of white wine together and I was hired to play that same night during the cocktail hour. The Canadian was a great connoisseur. He loved the accordion; he understood its blue-collar poetry and knew how to recognize truly skillful playing. His accordionist, the excellent Le Bordelais, was on leave, which had left the Canadian high and dry. Replacing Le Bordelais was no small task, as that stirring artist knew his instrument and had already earned the favor of the public: that of the bar and that of the streets. Be that as it may, I was to fill in for him as best I could. The Canadian became a friend. He was a loyal man, but one who could also take care of himself. In those days he was already famous. A French writer, Mr. Renaudin, had even written a book about the music-loving giant, a man who had known life's many struggles, and on fronts the whole world over. The same went for L'Oseille, his bartender. Among those good people, people whose lives seemed wonderfully colorful to me, I once again discovered the old Rouen of my youth, as it had been in those uncomplicated but harsh days when I had been as soft and as courteous as a pigeon.

"I lived fairly close to the Océanic Bar. I played during the cocktail hour and again in the evening at dinnertime. The clientele was not at all the sort where I hoped to find my fugitive monster. The people who frequented the Océanic belonged to a better world, one susceptible to the camaraderie of the night, a literary camaraderie whose dignity is contagious.

"During the day, I continued to search as best I could for this beast who, in the suburbs of Düsseldorf, had slit the throats of young girls. And I found nothing. But I liked my life at the Océanic Bar, and as long as possible, I prolonged that charming social position as a virtuoso accordionist by sending back fraudulent reports which were certain to keep my superiors' curiosity piqued.

"I went to bed at daybreak. I slept like the dead until nine o'clock. I would quickly go down and have a cup of coffee, smoke a cigarette, and then I would hurriedly go back up to my hotel room on Rue des Espagnols. Of course, I was living the life appropriate to my role. It wasn't always pleasant. I was then fifty years old and had picked up habits in keeping with my age and my comfortable financial situation.

"I can bend myself to any discipline. For that reason I pass fairly cheerfully through the surprises of an era in which no one is sure of his next meal or the roof over his head.

"As soon as I had finished my coffee, I would return to my room and lie down, smoking cigarettes. Then I would daydream. I was trying to be interested in my mission. My mission appealed to me in principle, but I knew I was wasting my time in Rouen. And yet Rouen affected me deeply. It was as if I had gotten caught up in the amicable inactivity of my nights. However, I devoted my reveries to my concerns as a criminal investigator. The Rouen police did not know me. I worked alone, which was not my usual habit. My mornings were haunted by the silhouettes of assassins, who were not all the same by any stretch of the imagination. The way I saw it, in our times, there were four masters of public terror, four filmmakers who made prodigiously vile movies. This is who I saw, in chronological order: Jack the Ripper, Landru, Haarmann, and X, the Butcher of Flehe with his procession of exsanguinated young ladies and little girls. Pretty little Lenzen and sweet Hamacher, dead and pallid, a finger held to their wan lips, bid me to follow them. The frail little murder victims whispered to me, 'Come with us, we'll show you der Mann who killed us.'

"At this moment in time, my dear friend, I can see myself as I was then, on my bed in the Hotêl des Vikings, my head bursting with bloody hypotheses, all of them quite awful. Jack, Landru, Haarmann, and X from Düsseldorf stood before me, defeated and treacherous like killers already caught up in the chain of events leading to their execution. Were they all still alive when the moment of their arrests finally came? It's a fact, at least for the last three. It is still quite difficult to wrap your head around it. Those four names belong to literature much more than they do to reality, at least for those who form an exceedingly restrained opinion of factual reality and of the social existence of man. Jack the Ripper, Landru, Haarmann of Hanover, and the mysterious killer of Düsseldorf all served the same master: the demon of secret thoughts. This incomparable, multifarious figure lends a constantly renewed youthfulness to the romanticism of the streets, the fields and the forest. He sometimes appears in the spectacle of the imagination like a cunning actor of little standing. He is deft, arrogant, lamentable, and spry. The facial traits which for others would simply be obscene—like the pallor of the skin—become for him the fundamental details of the clammy terror he inspires. His strength stems from his infamy and from the appallingly thoughtless cruelty of his instincts.

"The true incarnation of the man we called Jack the Ripper was the same as that of the character to whom Stevenson gave the name Edward Hyde. You are familiar with the strange tale of that bourgeois denizen split into two fundamental elements: that of evil and that of good. Jekyll is ignorant, during the day, of what Edward Hyde, his sinister double, envisions during the night. The retribution begins at precisely the moment when the two personalities of the same man are able to compare themselves to each other and to come to a mutual judgment. Perhaps Jack the Ripper disappeared, unpunished by man, the day he became fully aware of the indescribable compulsion that peopled his nights with disemboweled corpses.

"It appears that Jack the Ripper may have revealed his true identity before dying in some hospital or other in the United States. The mystery lives on, however, intact and inflated by horror and conjecture, just as it was, not so long ago, when he would send the working girls of Whitechapel scurrying home in fear as night fell. In those days, Whitechapel was still a notorious neighborhood, much like Montmartre, La Chapelle, and Belleville likely were some seventy years ago. It wasn't then the honest ghetto it is today, but a mass of sordid houses where misery, in a push to expedite damnation, created a vivid imagery that was almost unimaginable. The streetwalkers lived on Petticoat Lane and Houndsditch, between the Aldgate and the Bishopsgate. Petticoat Lane has since become Middlesex Street. But the police still remember Jack. They know that the large wooden carriage door on Durward Street encloses the courtyard where they found the body of the Ripper's first victim. That notorious monster brings to mind Wells's Invisible Man. He killed with a staggering quickness, then he melted away into the fog. He could choose between Mayfair and the low roads of Poplar to once again take his normal shape. Terror reigned in London's working-class neighborhoods. It was similar to the terror that makes

the girls and women of Düsseldorf shiver when the wind moans and howls, regardless of the reason. It bears witness to the gripping spectacles that unfold in those wastelands and solitary prairies haunted by the insomnia of the doers of Great Deeds.

"It is easy enough to imagine pretty much anything you want about Jack the Ripper. In my opinion, he was a more or less 'normal' man during the day. *His* night complete, perhaps he played the role of a good father, a good husband.

"Landru was a different story. That astonishing man knew how to keep his double hidden. The law convicted and guillotined a Landru who wasn't entirely the same as the man from the little house in Gambais. The Landru who lived in the nighttime must have transformed himself to the point where abomination ceased to have a precise meaning. That same Landru must have also heard the voices that mingled with that of the wind when it would set the lilacs of Gambais to swaying. I have heard tell of Landru's hands. A witness once told me what his thoughts had been, face to face with that man: this was a man who struggled against other men because of memories he couldn't manage to piece together. The lack of understanding between the justice system and the criminals is often staggering. Neither of them speaks the same language. Especially the criminals, who, when they are in the grips of erotic madness, find themselves in agony without really understanding what is befalling them. It is well understood that the law cannot concern itself with these details, because it is duty-bound to protect the community against all of the elements of mortification, whether the guilty party is following the flute or banging the drum.

"Landru, although everyone can still picture his face now that it has become so well known, remains a character of mystery, part of the criminal shadows. Such as he is now, he embodies order and the economy, two inoffensive but transposed virtues in a sphere where the blood is shed in clandestinity.

"Of course it would be Germany who would once again offer up a perfect companion for the mandrake, a plant ostensibly born of the final jerks of a hanged man. Haarmann, the Butcher of Hanover, and the murderer from the kermesse fairs of Düsseldorf. Hanover is a city where you can find a little of everything: opulent neighborhoods, the triumph of the reinforced concrete of the Romantic era, and those narrow streets where you could supposedly find the restaurants Haarmann furnished with human meat. A poor woman, when asked by the president of the tribunal whether or not she had bought meat from Haarmann, had replied, as if excusing herself, 'Oh no, we were too poor, we only bought pieces of bone for making soup.' The horrifying mysteries of life do not hide in the abysses, home to the blind fish, but instead in the yet unexplored depths of human misery, and they are difficult to fathom without having sacrificed a succession of things that we all consider to be essential. The most repugnant sort of scum gravitated around Haarmann, such as Dorchen, the little prostitute with the leprous scaliness of a fish, and Mr. Hans, a loathsome, homicidal little queer. He would be the one moaning behind the door as the butcher, worked up into a frenzy, was strangling his victim. 'Pay attention . . . ah, damn it, you're going to ruin the jacket again!' To really grasp the horror that people such as these can provoke, one must follow them right up until the moment when, their gaze untroubled and their desires satisfied, they are at rest, perhaps wandering a public promenade just like everyone else, strolling along beneath an honorable sun.

"Did this terrible maniac from Düsseldorf share in this same essence? To my belief, he surpassed them all. His madness raised him frightfully above any hypothesis one could formulate about a criminal. His cunning was beyond all comparison. His craftiness was not unlike that of those mental patients who, a few years ago, had found a means of opening all the safety locks of the asylum where they were imprisoned by using keys they made out of the tin from old food cans. The logic of the mad can surpass the limits of our feeble imaginations. The Düsseldorf killer's imagination was completely inhuman. It did not have the slightest connection to the standards men use when evaluating the quality of an imagination. Perhaps he was nothing but a tremendous fool with a benevolent side. Outside of that fatal instant when something gave way within him, during that moment when the poor master of the mental attic bent to that will, he might have been nothing more than an inoffensive cretin whose imagination toiled away without respite. It is often within the cement skull of the fool that the craziest adventures are born. Adventure! A word that is so often cursed. It is not upon the respectable paths of the tropical world, or even the arctic, that we can come up against our limits. Adventure lies within man. It knows no bounds. Blood is its terrifying revelation. Blood, which is a word of nobility, must yield in this case to the German word, 'Das Blut,' which is thicker, more tragic, richer in tainted imagery. 'Das Blut,' a creation of the wriggling maggots who nip at our heels in the small, nameless streets of those small, nameless towns that rule over the myriad incidents of midnight.

"This sort of thinking ought to alter the appearance of a policeman. That is not the case. We are no longer characters with exceptional exteriors. Policemen who are ruled by their imaginations make for lousy policemen. The true adventure that makes up policing is mechanical, and the majority of detective novels only tell their readers tales of mechanical adventure, or offer problems to their perspicacity, puzzles, riddles to solve that take place outside of real life.

"Living like this, among imaginary characters, I was gradually losing touch with reality. I could feel it distinctly. And it was from the port of Rouen that I was asking for a miracle: that of putting me in contact with universally recognized human values. When you live among ghosts, you can't live off the land. And so there is no need to travel. In Rouen, as in Naples, as in London, Brest, and Barcelona, I had arrived with my own ghosts. It was as if I had become the ringleader of a traveling circus. I had taken the reins of my own personal caravan of circus wagons crammed full of curiosities; I was setting up shop in the town square and putting my cabinet of curiosities on public display. Once the lights had gone out, I returned home with my marionettes and they imposed their lives and décor on me. In each European port to which my destiny steered me, whether in the crowd or in the solitude of my hotel room, I would once again find the same clowns, the same acrobats, the same high-wire walkers, the same trick horsemen, all the usual monsters of the human menagerie with the many jealousies that take place among them, the well-read bearded ladies, the lustful man-with-no-limbs, the hateful Siamese sisters, and the enraged five-legged sheep. In the middle of that stunted society, I was just another

Barnum: a poet Barnum, a spy Barnum, a Barnum of the police, a Barnum whose secret tastes tended more specifically toward lending some color to the game he was tracking. A killer whom I put on show became a circus freak, a celebrity for the headlining show on the main stage, under the big top. This wasn't really what I had been looking for when I had accepted money from society, which had entrusted me with its interests.

"One night, without saying my goodbyes, I vanished from the bar in Rue de la Savonnerie. In my bags I carried a few new souvenirs, some very old but rejuvenated souvenirs, a bundle of new songs that would be easy to retain. I whistled a tune that brought pain to my heart as I stood on the platform of a deserted train station, awaiting the train from Le Havre.

"I managed to slip unseen into a Pullman, which carried me toward Paris. The celebrated sight of the port of Rouen was played out one more time before my eyes. I did not take the time to rest in Paris. I was anxious to get back to Hamburg, my true home. I was returning empty-handed, but I was not overly concerned about what I would tell my superiors.

"I had learned an overwhelming song of a sentimental bitterness, one of those pretty street songs where everything blends together, where the love of young girls is matched by the divine importance of the streets. I played that waltz on my accordion. Should I play that song for my bosses and try to fetter them to my own memories? It seemed like an absurd idea to me. In Hanover, I took full responsibility for my investigative inactivity. I was richer by one song, a song sung to the melody of an old waltz . . .

"The sweetheart I had left behind in Rue de la Savonnerie was named Marcelle."

IX

THIRD VERSION OF THE DEATH OF BAMBÙ

"It was not Joan Labet who informed me about the exact end of Mrs. Anita Wood, otherwise and elsewhere known as Mlle Bambù, or Signorina Bambù. The matter," continued Captain Hartmann, "was recounted to me in Tétuàn, in the great hall of the Hotel Alphonse XIII, in the middle of a concert given by three dozen song canaries, the value of which would prove disconcerting for anyone not previously in the know as to the value of canaries.

"The man who told me of Anita Wood's end was a stout young man, his face scarred by smallpox. He was an anxious fellow, worked up about the various possible outcomes of the war; he seemed rather unsure of the ground on which he stood.

"Nothing I had managed to dig up about the likely end of Signorina Bambù, in truth just snippets of idle gossip, had been able to appease me. By way of that beautiful gold-skinned she-rogue, my own modest and violent youth called to me. A certain sense of morality had come to me along with my wealth. In those days, several weeks before my departure for Rouen, I was unaware, and of course without any ill will on my part, that there was such a thing as a social morality, the laws of which could at times be logical despite their severity.

"This young man who, some time after the death of Mrs. Anita Wood, had served with a *bandera* barracked up in the mountains in Chaouen, made it possible for me to reconstruct the final days of this woman who had been the little devil on my shoulder, but at the same time the poetic side of a large part of my life. As I smoked my pipe, scarcely distracted by the

virtuosity of the hotel's canaries, I was able to reconstruct the film in much more detail. And that is how, from one document to the next, it became possible for me to imagine and organize what follows, in order to rid my stories once and for all of the presence of that possessed half-Cuban, the activities of whom were quite truly devilish.

"I knew where she had lived. Her schemes fed on the riotous Ramblas. I had only to close my eyes to see it ... It was a typical summer's night, rich with the heady scent of the canna. From her window, opened wide to the cheerful murmur that rose up from the city, Mademoiselle Alice Z., a Martinican who danced in a club on the Paralelo, contemplated the ramblas and the lights of Plaça de Catalunya. A concerned and melancholy crease at the corners of her lips gave her the face of a pouty young woman.

"Mlle Alice's mission as a double agent in the service of France was drawing to a close. Her mission happily fulfilled, all she had left to do was transport the documents to France, a few thin sheets of onionskin paper, astutely hidden. Which was not as easy as it sounds. In a few hours, Alice would board the train. She would finally have an idea of the chances of her success when she reached the station in Girona.

"The young woman was apprehensive, irritated. She moved about restlessly. She closed the window to the noise of the trams and the hum of the crowd that packed the renowned boulevard in front of the theater. A few hours remained before sundown; her train was to depart at a little before six in the morning. It was midnight ... My information is specific but correct.

"Mlle Alice knew she would not be able to sleep. She picked up a newspaper and tried her best to read it. The letters danced before her eyes. She thought she heard the sound of cautious footsteps in the stairwell and on the landing in front of her door. She got up, listening carefully, and took up a small automatic pistol that was concealed beneath one of the divan cushions.

"She no longer heard anything. Still armed, she opened the apartment door. The landing was empty. Leaning over the banister to look down into the stairwell, she noted nothing suspicious on the level below.

"She returned to sit down; and the events of the days she had just so dangerously lived through played over and over in her mind like a film whose strange reality she couldn't quite manage to follow. She had succeeded in breaking into the safe of the head of German Intelligence, of which she was the somewhat tarnished star. She had absconded with some ciphers, and it was that precious sheet of paper she had to get to France before the end of the following day, as, upon the return of Von whatever-his-name-was in a few hours, the theft would not take long to be discovered. It was during that man's absence, while he was away in Ceuta, that Mlle Alice had been able to carry out the burglary she had been planning for over a year. Everyone thought her to be in the service of Germany, and Alice had suffered a great deal from the attitudes of those around her. One must drink the cup of bitterness to the very dregs: suffer and serve. One woman, just one, had shown her friendship. Her name was Anita Wood. She was also a woman of color. But much as was the case with Mlle Alice, her skin was light and golden. Alice was uncertain of the nationality of this supple dancer who said she was Martinican. It was possible. She was a devoted friend, of little apparent curiosity: a frivolous and sensual woman, tall and lithe much as Alice was herself. Their figures were those of two sisters. Yet one of them, Alice, was blonde in spite of her mixed blood, while Mrs. Anita Wood was a brunette. Alice had never confided in her. She knew to be distrustful and was well aware of the sudden and very permanent dangers of her profession. Without ever being able to find a good reason, she always tensed up somewhat when Anita appeared next to her, smiling and without a sound. 'You make less noise than a mouse,' Alice would say. Anita Wood would laugh softly and offer no reply. Mlle Alice had not forewarned Anita of her departure.

"'Never trusting anyone,' mused Alice, 'is enough to harden your heart.'

"At that moment, her doorbell rang. The young woman leapt to her feet and took up the pistol, which she slid into her bodice. With a resolute step, she opened the door, the security chain of which had been fastened.

"'Oh, it's you, Anita. Come in.'

"Anita was not smiling. She stepped inside, and Mlle Alice saw that she held a suitcase in her hand.

"Anita seemed shaken. Alice made her sit down.

"'What is it?' she asked.

"'I'm going to tell you, Alice . . . I'm a member of the Intelligence Service, and I'm leaving in the morning, because I know from a reliable source that my cover has been blown here. You know what that means . . . sooner or later . . .'

"'Ah! You're with the Intelligence Service?'

"'Yes, I apologize for never having said anything to you, but mistrust is part of the job: an occupational hazard.'

"'Ah!' repeated Alice.

"She thought for a moment, and then turning quickly, she said, 'You see, I understand, as I myself am working for German Intelligence.'

"Great surprise showed on Anita's face, and Mlle Alice looked at her curiously without it being possible for her friend to tell what she was thinking or to spot the anxiety that had rendered her nearly speechless.

"All of this lasted only two or three minutes, and then Mlle Alice declared: 'I too am leaving for France in a few hours. Why don't we travel together?'

"'That would be comforting,' replied Anita.

"'Excuse me, my dear. I'm going to have to leave you on your own. I've already dismissed my maid. Stay right where you are. Don't open the door to anyone . . . You're safe here in this apartment. I'll be back in an hour. I need to show myself in order to dispel any suspicion.'

"Mlle Alice put her hat on, kissed her friend, and after recommending one final time that she not open the door, closed and double-locked the door behind her. Then she noisily made her way down the two flights of stairs. She slammed the door to the street, and, as quietly as a wolf, she climbed back up the two flights she had just descended. Softly, she opened a secret door that led into a small, dark closet from where she could see what was going on in the large apartment where she had left Anita, alone and disheartened, slumped across the divan like a discarded sweater. Thanks to a craftily installed peephole, Alice saw what she wanted to see and made certain of that which she needed to know for a fact.

"The face of that woman of mixed race, transformed, had become the face of a woman full of hostility, nastiness, and cunning. With what seemed like a great deal of experience, she was delicately rummaging through the suitcase Anita had packed. Then, disappointed, she worked her way around the room. With precision, a precision that filled Alice's heart with a wave of terror, she examined certain objects . . . the hollow candles atop the piano, the pendulum of a small clock, and the porcelain doorknob. Anita unscrewed it. It was empty. She put it back in place and bit her lip.

"Mlle Alice had seen enough. She slipped out just as quietly, silently making her way back down the stairs. Once she was outside, she began to run. She stopped in a quiet little street, in front of curiosity shop. It was open.

"'Hello, Paul,' she said.

"'Have you something important to tell me?' he asked.

"'Yes,' said Alice, 'death is in the air.'

"'You can speak freely, we're alone here. If someone comes into the shop, haggle over that handbag.'

"And so Alice told him what she had seen in her apartment.

"'You did the right thing in coming here,' Monsieur Paul replied calmly. 'An hour ago, I learned from D. 55 that an offensive had been organized against a French agent, in the high-speed to Paris. I had thought it to be a joke. I was unaware you had to leave this morning . . . After everything you have told me, I believe that you're in danger. Don't leave this morning.'

"'It is absolutely necessary that I leave this morning,' replied Alice. 'Still,' she continued, 'what you might be able to do . . . Dispatch two reliable men on the six o'clock train, ready for anything . . . They will see to throwing a little scare into my travel companion during the trip . . .'

"'You've got a companion?'

"'Yes, the most dangerous spy currently in the service of Germany.'

"'Good heavens!' he exclaimed.

"She went on: 'Your two agents, I repeat, will give a fright to my girlfriend, letting her know that she has been made . . . Good. Now, here is the most important part. Send your big Mercedes to Girona with two of your best men. These men mustn't hesitate to do away with the woman who gives them the correct password: "Turtle dove." She must be eliminated. The woman will likely be dressed as I am right now. Yes, if all goes well . . . If things don't go well, no one will get off at Girona. If so, have your car and your men leave immediately. Farewell!'

"'Farewell, and may luck be on your side! All will be executed according to your instructions,' at which point Monsieur Paul likely looked at his watch and picked up the telephone receiver."

At this stage of his tale, Captain Hartmann interrupted himself, perhaps to prepare for the impact of its conclusion. He soon launched back in:

"Finally they were alone in the compartment. Mlle Alice was the first to speak.

"'It is known, my dear Anita, that I am working for the Germans. Thus I will not be able to cross the French border. I will get off in Girona, where a car is waiting to take me across by a secret route. Two men will be waiting for me at the station! The password is "turtle dove." I cannot ask you to come with me, as these men, knowing that you are in the service of the Allies, would definitely grab you. They have my description, as they have never laid eyes on me before. They are aware that I am of color and how I am currently dressed. There. This must be where our destinies take us in different directions.'

"'I could simply denounce you,' Anita said coldly.

"'No, my dear,' Alice replied, 'for your cover here would be blown . . . We both know where we stand and we're both in the same situation . . . and what's more, I'm quite fond of you. You've never done me wrong.'

"'That is true,' said Anita Wood.

"'All I ask of you,' added Alice, 'is to keep a close eye on our car. There are too many people, including some men of whom the both of us ought to be wary.'

"Anita suppressed a smile.

"'You're right,' she said.

"She disappeared down the hallway, as Mlle Alice, standing in front of her compartment, watched her recede from view down the corridor.

"She remained like that for over half an hour. Then, from where she stood, she could see Anita, her back against the door that led to the next car.

Anita seemed to be listening attentively. Mlle Alice walked toward her. However, she turned back the way she had come and went into her compartment, as Anita, with an urgent gesture, had signaled her to stop advancing.

"She did not wait long. Mrs. Wood entered the compartment. Her face was pale. She spoke plainly.

"'I'm going to die . . . There are two men who have been sent to kill me. What can I do? I won't make it across the French border.'

"'There's only one way,' said Mlle Alice, 'just one: Let's trade clothes. In my suitcase, there is a blonde wig. Put it on . . . The color of our skin, by a stroke of luck, makes us look like sisters. As for me, I have nothing to worry about. My papers are in order and I will identify myself at the border. It wasn't in my plans, because a car was to be waiting for me in Girona. The men tasked with getting me across the border know my description and the password, which is "turtle dove." You'll take my place and you will be saved . . . Quickly, let's change clothing, we'll be at the border in an hour.'

"In all haste, but with efficient and precise movements, they exchanged clothing. With a few snips of the scissors, Anita's black hair came off. Alice threw it behind the curtain. Anita Wood put on the blonde wig. With it on, she looked nearly identical to her companion.

"The two women looked at each other with a smile. Then Anita took a small mirror from her bag and painstakingly looked herself over. 'Extraordinary,' she said as she tucked the mirror away. And the two of them waited, neither saying a word.

"Outside, it was raining. The rain streamed down the windowpanes. In the corridor, two suspicious men came and went outside the door to the compartment. The train came to a halt at Girona. Without a word, Anita got down, suitcase in hand. Alice didn't spare her a glance. A car door slammed shut and the train resumed its journey."

Captain Hartmann stopped once again. He offered me a cigarette. "Now where was I," he said. He feigned a rather mundane indifference and continued with his story.

"The anticipated automobile drove on through the gray and gloomy day. The mountains seemed to press down upon it. From afar, the car seemed to climb along the edge of the precipice like a stubborn beetle. Anita Wood watched the doleful scenery and, in front of her, the backs of the two men: the driver and his companion.

"Some time later, the rain redoubled its intensity and the car came to a halt. One of the men got out and opened the rear door.

"'Mademoiselle, would you please step out of the car. We have taken a wrong turn, and in order to double back, my friend must perform a difficult maneuver. Please get out, it would be more prudent.'

"Anita Wood stepped out. Her legs, numb from the cold, were shaky. She did not have time to see her death approach.

"She felt the cold of a metal object against her neck and immediately crumpled without crying out. The detonation of the automatic pistol sent forth echo after echo.

"The man, pistol smoking in his hand, waited for the noise to subside. He lifted the young woman's body and threw it into the ravine; then he once again took his seat in the car, its engine humming softly . . .

"Was that me who was just speaking?" asked Captain Hartmann. "I no longer even recognize the sound of my own voice."

He vacantly tapped the end of a cigarette against the back of his hand. Then he slid it into his pocket.

"It's as clear-cut as a police report," he said. "No embellishments, no added local color. That is what you call a quick end, in the truest sense of the words, or a death without pity, for the poets of a certain age such as myself. Thus Anita Wood, or perhaps more appropriately Signorina Bambù, met such an end for having found a shoe that fit, which is to say for having found another person with the same charms as hers, but even more clever."

Captain Hartmann took the cigarette from his pocket and lit it.

"Many people are afraid of living," he said. "They are not as naïve as they might seem."

X

THE CAPTAIN'S SENTIMENTAL END

"Once again, here I am in Hamburg. This time I am free. Free? Perhaps, but at least liberated from any professional obligations. There is no point in relating to you, detail by detail, the source of my wealth. Tales like that one are only of interest to those who profit from them. Anyways, it is banal, as I have told you. A relative, one of my father's brothers with whom I had lost touch, made sure to provide me with a very pleasant future. What that future is worth, by weight and volume, I do not know. I am wealthy, certainly rich enough for what time I have left to live, which is to say, for an optimist, a decade at best. Ten diabolically brief years. I have already been ensnared by the rapid descent toward the end. As have you, for that matter.

"Anyway, I have now been living here for roughly three months, in this comfortable hotel which is more or less a city put together in a film studio. I adore this thoroughfare from which I can catch a glimpse of the Binnenalster, every bit as poetic as the Lac d'amour in Bruges. I am shown a great deal of respect. They refer to me as Captain Hartmann, which is truly the name that best suits me, for I am a captain of anxiety and of secretive goings-on. Several generations were born amidst the vague and informal poetry that preceded the war. All of that actually came to an end when your Moulin Rouge caught fire. That was the first disaster of the Great War, in the sense that it signaled the end of a certain form of the poetry of the streets. The radiance given off by that girl and her mack, her Lùdwig, still reaches us today, still moves us and us alone, even if the source of that radiance died in the fire. The destruction of the Moulin Rouge was equivalent to an *auto-da-fé* involving hundreds of books. Nowadays, the sentimental value of those books has gone out of date. And it hurts me, as it must also hurt you, even though you are younger than me, I suppose, by about ten years. I am happy to have met you in Hamburg, which is a Hanseatic city, and a frank city, by which I mean a city where opinions and emotions are shared with frankness.

"This is why I have chosen Hamburg in order to attempt an experiment in liberation. I have succeeded. And you might be the only one who will understand that this was not without a terrible sundering of both the intellect and the heart.

"Here, before the piers of Saint Pauli, my personality has been obliterated. Now I am nothing more than a man, a candidate for death, just like all the other men who enter into this period of concession that precedes annihilation.

"By settling in a hotel in the Neuer Jungfernstieg, my wallet fully stocked, sheltered from the financial wizards, I was once again the old man formerly of Naples, Palermo, London, Barcelona, and Rouen. Well-dressed and sober, my appearance no longer disgusted me when I would chance upon a glimpse of it in a mirror.

"It was with delight that I inhaled the fog of the Alster and the Bille, mingled with the thick smoke escaping from the many steamships on the Northern Elbe. The Flemish charm of the old town calmed my nerves, weary from the deviousness of policing and espionage. I loved to hear this city's hard talk and I was savoring the adventure, my own adventure, along the Seemannstrasse, passing the ship chandler's shops filled with the accessories of my own particular melancholy. Smoking a cigar, for a man of my age, is a pleasure that climbs a few steps up the scale of sensual values. I didn't know a soul in this town. This pleased me and pandered to my taste for the unknown in all its forms, on the sole condition that they be social in nature. I would chat with the hotel doorman, with the bartender, and my chambermaid, who was lissome, elegant, and exceedingly proper ... Always proper ...

"One day as I was smoking at my window, a little before the evening twilight, I got the feeling that a renewed strength was rejuvenating my skin, my face, my eyes, my slackened lips. I looked at myself in the mirror and I liked what I saw. And with some surprise, too, for just the night before my face had appeared drab to me, wrinkled and underhandedly senile. Humming to myself, I donned a light gray three-piece suit made of a smooth, warm fabric, a suit that was very simple and very costly. I put on a hat of the same material, and having slipped on a raincoat, I left home, my eyes bright, my nose curious, and my muscles ready for all possible relaxations. Of course, it was raining. The bellboy was about to rush out in search of a car when, motioning with my arm, I stopped him in his tracks. No, no. Looking this sharp, I was not about to lock myself away inside a vile, sequestering taxi. I was young and I wanted fresh air, the rain on my overcoat, on my face. I wanted to hear all the sounds of the Elbe, the grinding of the trams and, most importantly, the sound of my own footsteps on the sidewalks.

"The collar of my raincoat flipped up, I went down toward Herrlichkeit Street, shivering with pleasure. It felt as if my body was brushing against everything in the street. I stopped to look at the lovely typists on their way home from work. All of the streetlamps were reflected in the water of the canal and on the slick asphalt. Night had fully arrived and was enveloping Hamburg, the Hamburg of work, of poetry, of gangsters, of millionaire thugs followed by their bodyguards. An American way of life that stretched all the way to Marseille, where the gangsters also occupy the top rung of the good life afforded by midnight.

"I pulled out my watch, a lovely piece which I no longer possess. It was seven o'clock. I was hungry, and it was a healthy, juvenile hunger. A simple restaurant was all I needed to satisfy it. I wanted to eat unhindered, without the singular attitude one takes on when eating in front of the maître d', the waiters and sommeliers, the men and women at the neighboring tables in formal suits and evening gowns. I hailed a taxi, which softly glided to a stop before me, almost like an accomplice. 'Take us,' I said, 'toward Saint Pauli. You can drop me off in the Schmuckstrasse when I knock on the panel.'

"The automobile rolled through the night like a chauffeur-driven luxury car, lit by the occasional flashes of the trams, passing alongside other cars that gave me the impression they were full of life, youthful and mysterious. I was still humming, as the particular song fit my jubilation. 'Love

comes, love goes . . .' I pictured myself, accordion on my knees, drawing all the mischievous rhythms of the street toward me, apportioning tender alms of an unrivaled sentimentality to each young working girl. With each turn of the wheels that carried me farther into the working-class neighborhoods, I found, once again, the scent of my youth, and that of the girls who conserved that delicate poetry, like a lilac branch, a branch heavy with those touching little lilacs that grow in city suburbs. I had the taxi stop before a cheerful, unassuming-looking restaurant. For no particular reason, I decided I would dine there, because a surge of youthfulness was guiding me and because I felt like casually mixing with the nightlife in the way I had when I was twenty years old, along the marina in Naples.

"I sat down at a table near the bay window, which afforded me a view of the street. There were few guests: port workers, for the most part. Across from me sat a small brunette, quite Polish-looking, a young woman with gentle eyes who was eating quietly without a glance for her surroundings. Even so, she noticed me, and since I was smiling at her, she responded in kind. She got up, her meal concluded, and left. I hurried to pay and I saw her waiting a little ways farther down, by the corner. She stood watching for me under the rains. I asked her if she would keep me company for the rest of the evening, and she accepted. 'My name is Lia, and I am Polish,' she said. 'And you?'

"'You can call me Captain Hartmann,' I said, 'and don't you worry; the night will be good to the both of us.'

"'Let's take a taxi to the Eden,' she added.

"'No,' I told her, 'let's walk, if you don't mind; walk, and I will buy you new shoes. But tonight, I want to go everywhere. Everywhere you'll find friends and everywhere I might too. I know how life is, Lia, on that you can trust me . . . In the old days, I lived here, between the Marktplatz and the Reeperbahn. Nothing will catch me by surprise, because, or at least so I presume, nothing has changed. Even you, Lia, you look just like all the young girls I knew here before I left.'

"'Africa? America?' questioned Lia. And without awaiting my reply, she added: 'I know a *Lokal*, it isn't far from here . . .'

"'Lia, first let's wander the Reeperbahn. It isn't raining. Leave your umbrella, which doesn't suit you . . . I'll reimburse you for it.' I was already acting as if we were old friends.

"She didn't want to abandon her umbrella. I slipped a bill inside her glove. She carefully set down her umbrella in the corner of a doorway. She sighed. She visibly regretted that ridiculous accessory.

"We entered a large dance hall where it was possible to telephone minor improprieties from one table to another with impunity. Lia was uncomfortable. Her small pantsuit, cut of a light, navy-blue cloth, seemed a bit skimpy. But under her little felt cloche, she was as good as any one of them, because she was small, sweet, and young, unquestionably young. Some women suggested amorous combinations to her by telephone. Lia recovered her self-assurance. She drank some champagne, her cheeks grew quite pink, and she began to sing to herself, purring away. That hot, extravagant club proved to be extremely mediocre. I paid the check. Lia followed me toward the cloakroom. I already felt a bit cloudy from the champagne I had drunk.

"'There, there, child, hold your head high, walk confidently, you're better than anyone in here.'

"The woman at the coat check scornfully looked Lia over from head to toe. My little Pole seemed truly intimidated. That night she leapfrogged over ten years of her life and unwittingly ended up in the imposing world of old men and ardent old women covered in jewelry. All of that proper, congested world must have seemed terribly outdated to her. As for me, thanks to the champagne that was already affecting me, I was infiltrating the world of the young, one long stride at a time.

"Lia suggested a cabaret that she knew well because her friends went there at night after work. She did not say what work they did. It was in the Langestrasse, I believe, that we discovered the door to that Eden. A cellar door half buried in the earth. The stench of chicken bouillon wafted tepidly through an open door guarded by a rather robust doorman, fanned along by comings and goings through a hallway door that was set below street level.

"'That's it,' my companion said to me.

"We entered, preceded by a waitress. Every head turned our way. At the center of the room, four accordions whimpered softly, waiting for silence to be restored before the arrival of the singer. We sat down at a table. Lia ordered champagne. She felt at home here. She regained some of her professional authority. The singer made her way into the circle of light splayed out on the floor at the feet of the four accordionists, who then opened with a prelude of powerful chords, the sounds of which moved me deeply. And right away, the singer, who looked like Maria Ney, launched into an old song: *In Sankt-Pauli bei Altona . . .*

"The room applauded, and the accordions launched into a famous waltz, the Seemantlos Waltz. The singer had taken up a megaphone and her raw but moving voice defiled us from head to toe. Lia beat her hands together and I raised my glass in honor of the singer, Scilly Schwarz. Oh, everything was starting over, like it was before: the same men, the same women, the same songs. I kept drinking and a thousand lights lit up inside my head. I had become a radio receiver, but one built to receive long-dead waves.

"Lia sang quietly, swinging her legs like a little girl. She was hungry. We drank some chicken bouillon, we ate some oysters, sausages, and slices of buttered brown bread. And we drank. I held on to the bottle as I had long ago, with the Bersaglieri at Signorina Bambù's table, with the Swiss in Barcelona, the sailors in Limehouse, and L'Oseille, the Canadian's bartender.

"'Hey there!' I shouted at them. 'Sing for me! No, let me sing you the song of the 1st Foreign in 1906 . . . Youpaïda, youpaïda! No, wait . . . Ah!'

"My memory no longer obeyed my enthusiasm. The accordionists, who at first seemed to encourage me, were now packing their instruments into cases lined with red flannel.

"A choir of robust longshoremen in the back of the room, next to the lavatory, gradually got to their feet and raised their voices. One of them shouted: 'Bel Abbès . . . You'll get your *boudin*!'

"And then they sang a new song that was popular all the way from Gueliz to Bel Abbès, several of them whistling in imitation of the fifes.

"'That, old man, is Bu Denib, Midelt, the Road to Ziz.'

"The man sniggered. Some shipwrights sporting top hats and wearing bottle-green velvet got up to leave. One of them, on his way past Lia, lifted her chin with a finger.

"The song I had just heard had plunged me into a sorrow that came down on me like a roundhouse.

"'Drink up,' my young friend said to me.

"I drank two more glasses of wine.

"'You aren't talking anymore,' Lia observed. 'Why not?'

"We were alone in the cabaret, and by alone, I mean Lia the Polish girl, me, and a young man with a thin face who, his hands buried deep in the pockets of his pants, was looking at us with commiseration. He looked to be equal parts timid and parched.

"'Lia,' I said, 'ask that man if he wants to drink with us.'

"She gave a little sign and the young man came over and sat at our table. The waitress brought more wine, wine that was starting to sicken me, but wine that I wanted to drink because the menace of old age could only be vanquished by mighty slugs from a bottle. I was able to get over it and began talking again . . . I no longer have any idea what I spoke about. Oh yes! I said to that young man, 'You're very fortunate to have crossed my path on your journey. Don't say a thing, no reason to protest . . . You've lost hope, as I had at your age, sitting at a table without a drink before me, in a cabaret that I considered to be shelter . . . You and Lia, you are both a long-past day taken from my life . . . I had just now been trying to find the melody to the song in my memory that best describes that day.'

"The young man poured me another glass of sparkling wine. He tipped back his hat and said, 'Another bottle, mister?' He ordered.

"Lia applied some fresh red to her lips. A ghastly dawn began to hint at its arrival. My strength gave out. I could no longer fight the old age that now forced its way into my mind and body like an unstoppable whirlwind, sweeping from my memory the images that allowed me to resist.

"'We're going to go to Edwige's,' said the young woman.

"The woman from the cloakroom brought us our overcoats. Lia demanded her umbrella . . . The man gently pushed me into the hall, toward the street. Outside, it was still night. It was January; it could have been five in the morning.

"'Let's go to Edwige's,' repeated Lia.

"The two of them were holding me up, each of them taking me by one of my arms. I am pretty certain it was raining . . . I haven't the faintest idea how things unfolded after that.

"Later, much later, a Schupo found me sprawled out in a storage shed near the fish market. I was shivering. 'What are you doing there?' My age and my suit inspired a certain respect in him.

"'Come on . . . Time to go home!'

"He whistled down a taxi, put me in it, and repeated the address I gave him. 'Have you checked your wallet?' he asked me once again.

"'Yes,' I said to him, 'thank you . . . I haven't anything left. I have spent it all. Thank you very much.'

"Once in the car, I noted that I had been utterly divested of everything that had been in my pockets. My wristwatch had also disappeared.

"But nothing could offset the terrible grief I was feeling. Nothing, nothing! For at that moment, good sir, I understood all too well that I would never again cross paths with little Lia or that young man who had reminded me of myself when I was twenty years old. I returned to my hotel, swollen with emptiness. The doorman paid the taxi driver as I no longer had a penny on me. But it wasn't the stolen money that I lamented. My affluence was well above such a vulgar misadventure. Still, tell me, kind sir, and tell it to me straight: Are you certain that I will never again encounter little Lia and the young man who robbed me, who looked like I did at twenty years old? Are you certain that I won't meet them again, not here, not in Palermo, nor in London, nor in Rouen, nor in Barcelona, nor . . . ?"

"It seems to me that it's all over with now," I replied. "I think you can sleep easy."

January 1932

PÈRE BARBANÇON

I

REMINISCENCES OF THE GANGS

Paris, without electricity, became the prey of the nighttime. Infrequent yet unsettling talk occasionally disturbed the perfidious silence of the city, whose streets, like poorly ventilated pipes, groped their way along toward seedy nightmares.

After calling around to no avail from a random second-rate cabaret in hopes of finding a room in a hotel, I entered the night, exposed, to worm my way between its various dangers in the direction of the door of a hotel in Montmartre-le-Haut, on Rue Cortot, I believe, or perhaps Rue des Saules. In any case, at the summit of the butte Montmartre, frozen in the ebonite block of a night somewhere around 1942 or 1943. These details are largely unimportant. What is important, however, is to situate the setting of this story, one which is connected to those of Signorina Bambù and Captain Hartmann by way of the presence of Père Barbançon who, once upon a time in Rouen, had taught me the rudimentary principles of the poetry of the streets: those same streets which were haunted by cats, rats, and the novice sisters of the Order of the Cloche.

The hotel that opened up its doors to me was ancient; its exceedingly Napoleon III style led one to associate it with that of Manet's ladies in white, seated behind the delicate guardrail of a balcony of unforgettable simplicity. The woman who opened the door to me was definitely not wearing white. Truth be told, it was not a woman at all, but instead an elderly night porter armed with the butt of a candle stood up on the metal lid of an old-fashioned Balto cigarette tin. He led me to my room, the windows of

which opened onto the street. Then, after of course wishing me a good night, he left me alone with my stump of a candle, whose wick swam in a small pond of fetid grease. After which, the wick went out and it was night.

It was necessary for me to wrestle with the furniture to get into the bed. Fatigue prevented me from falling asleep right away. Lying on my back with my hands under my neck, I listened to the night and the spiteful footsteps of its patrols; the humming of an alarming engine.

My presence in that Montmartre hotel seemed anachronistic to me. Traces of my youth could be read in the darkness of that room. During nights spent in such hotels, exhausted by thoughts of lost time, I yearned for the dreamless sleep of the animals. It was on such a night that the word "gangs," in the plural, quite naturally popped into my head: the gangs of Montmartre, and the gangs of Rouen, of which Père Barbançon had been a part well before he knew Signorina Bambù.

It was not a question, in that particular evocation, of the gangs of Picardy, with their red flag and its white cross, nor of the gangs of Piedmont with their black flag decorated by a similar cross. The infantry, the French "companies of adventure," as they were officially known in the sixteenth century, were somewhat akin to the gangs whose memory was haunting me. Similar in that they had divided themselves into gangs from either above or below the Seine, much like the others split into two groups based at the top or the bottom of the slopes. That is where the comparison ends. Not, however, without leaving behind some fairly distinct imagery in the memories of those who had been involved.

Montmartre, naturally, was home to the gangs north of the Seine, the same way those from Rue du Pot-de-Fer were dependent on the Latin Quarter. Incidentally, both sides aligned themselves with Villon, whom Marcel Schwob had recently situated within a context that provided us with certain parallels to our own circumstances. This was a fragile condition, and at this juncture, from where I am writing, one that seems more or less incomprehensible. Its imagery was undeniable. God only knows how the art of painting managed to recruit so many volunteers who were so poorly informed about the demands of that beautiful vocation. To be completely honest, there were no schools that could sustain such enthusiasm

and such a great number of misconceptions. The companions making up those gangs, some of them came from provincial high schools, others arrived from an obscure period of their lives, enigmatic but devoid of joy, one which had nevertheless nourished a sense of hope strong enough to reduce them all to a shared denominator, a denominator which nonetheless remained uncommon.

In the narrow lanes of Montmartre, the gaiety of which was unalloyed, the education allowed for by truancy was conducted in the open air, in the wind of the Montmartre streets which scattered those students of fortune at the break of day once their lessons were over. Among those young men were those who were writing their dissertation on the experiences of midnight, earning degrees in imagination beneath a Latin moon that applied makeup to the pallid faces of resuscitated Lesbias. Some only knew Catullus or Apuleius through the perpetual acquiescence of the girls those poets had immortalized: of the past, they accepted nothing but the sentimental currency whose usage had not been abolished by law. That lyrical money could be exchanged in Rue Saint-Vincent much as it had been in the days when its palisade still stood, covered in rather vulgar graffiti. There you would find, with a bearing of visible indolence and a pipe between their teeth, the apprentice painters of Roger's gang and those of Milo's, who would paint the lilacs of Rue Cortot in the most doleful shades of pink. Usually, the leader of a gang had an atelier. There, with a precocious charisma, he could gather together the many elements of the group. No one would say, "so and so is from Jerome's atelier," but rather, "so and so is in Marcel's gang." The members of a gang would get together to talk and take refuge from the weather, or go to the café, or cross the Pont des Arts to reach the refuge of the Rue du Pot-de-Fer gang, whose leader's name no longer comes to mind; he was a cheerful, myopic sculptor who wore velvet the color of old gold and a pair of boots.

I did not enjoy reliving those days. They were dangerous times, and chance decided each of our lots. Chance governed our daily lives; it took care of the details, and not without malice. Chance, in a drunken frenzy, made the rounds of our resting formation like a pagan god driven from Mount Olympus, a cockatrice on the outside but a chicken on the in. Those

frenzied flights of fantasy were so fruitless that they were never able to produce anything good. The only traces of these gangs that still exist can be found in the mortified imaginations of the few companions who were able to overcome the obstacles planted before them in that colorless and clamorous night. Later, much later, the foreign colony inhabiting Montparnasse was able to reconstruct a blurry image of the former gangs of Montmartre. The middling deeds of that example of humanity, shaped by constant hunger and liquor, could comprise the chapters of a didactic work entitled "A Universal History of Desperation."

It is necessary to have perpetrated a great number of asininities, perhaps even irreparable in their makeup, for one to feel the need to write a book that can be considered unmitigated public confession.

In those days, the young men in the gangs who were my contemporaries absorbed life the same way a sponge absorbs the many liquids staining the tables of the bars at dawn. There were some so classic, among those liquids, that they rapidly evoked the garden of Greek roots and the pavilion where the military music of Olympus played from four to five the day of the Dionysian celebrations.

One might think, and not without some bitterness, that such a beginning for the great art galleries and the noble publishing houses lacked distinction. Showing the works of the Rue Saint-Vincent gang, publishing the first books of those of the Rue Ravignan gang, neither of these filled the publishers and art dealers with enthusiasm. It truly was a case of getting off to a poor start.

From the men of the *Mercure de France* or the *Revue Blanche*, you would never hear, "They're the ones from Jarry's gang, or Jules Laforgue's." A number of those aristocrats did, however, have interactions with the gangs themselves, thanks to the lack of privacy in the furnished hotels and the mediocrity of the meals therein, often considered to be an adventure in themselves.

Might it simply be the case that that designation to which we had grown accustomed was a product of our fusion in those streets, akin to magic melting pots capable of transforming the most lackluster metals into gold? It is possible. In the time of the gangs, which spawned burlesque

conquests that I no longer welcome, material concerns governed our spirits and trained them like circus horses. Our minds, tormented by the hope of idyllic meats, obliged us to complete our studies in the schools of the street, schools which very rarely confer diplomas. As comrades in the gangs based below the Seine, you were often genuinely green fruit, and the awareness of unattainable maturity came to you quite early. Those who were able to break away from that indocile herd, whether girls or boys, were not playing the game fairly. The string that held together the beads of the rosary was not all that solid. One after another, those strings broke; the beads rolled across the ground, where some of them took seed and ended up flowering and ripening according to the natural laws that preside over both seeds and ideas.

There is no point now in attempting to gather together the images of those who served for a short year or two in those juvenile gangs. Even a fairly serious inquiry would do nothing more than reinforce the misconception that inspired those appearances.

I believe it is still better to conflate both man and object, within the now delicate backdrop of the streets, the tender indulgence of which they never tired.

To be honest, those who best resisted the subtle yet disastrous influences of the street were those who were immunized by classical culture. The discipline needed for Latin declensions could win out over the nocturnal assaults of a freedom that was far too playful. A young student of Latin is never lacking in grace. The gangs of Montmartre were home to many young Latin students who knew by rote the many japes of Antiquity capable of renewing tradition. This tradition, in turn, was that of the considerable path followed by schoolchildren, the longest of them all, which, from one school to the next, from bathhouse to cabaret and from street to street, led these predestined young men toward their true characters. For this very reason, that vocation came tardily. There were no child prodigies in the gangs. The most gifted rarely even bothered with self-discovery. Along they went like ambulatory sponges, soaking up rivers of song, absurd hypotheses, uninspired adventures, all without it dawning on them that one day down the road, some of them would be able to squeeze that sponge and have a mixture gush forth capable of feeding a talent that often turned out to be genuine.

Thus the film that was my life played out in crisp images, cut off from the many exploits of Hartmann, Signorina Bambù, and Père Barbançon, who may not have fully revealed the lasting sorrow of my thoughts, both literary and otherwise. Outside of the lusterless confessions of the aged Hartmann, I had not heard any further talk of Père Barbançon. Not once, since the age of twenty-three, had I laid eyes on Père Barbançon, who was perhaps not even the same Père Barbançon as that of Captain Hartmann. To be honest, the two characters had begun to merge together. Since that last encounter with the nimble gunman of Limehouse, I had acquired the experience of the streets and that of the military camps. Indeed! To the gangs of 1902, the vestiges of which I had just revisited, were subsequently added the battalions of Nancy in 1914. The inexorable march through lost time progressed logically. The gangs of Montmartre found each other once again in the military forts of Toul or Dongermain. A fine summer's day brought with it the smells of Rue Saint-Vincent and the road to Écrouves. Rose Blanche, from Rue des Saules, carried the rifle of a man from the gang who had entrusted all his ambitions to his regiment of the colonial infantry. The lilacs from my father's gardens blossomed on the lips of the demoiselles in Nancy: a perfectly distinctive marching song was born in order to rejuvenate the repertoire of the barracks. At the time, we knew that it was coming into being, but the lyrics were never written down.

Those in the gangs who knew how to write wrote, and some of them nobly. But the tune of that song from Nancy was lost the same way the time was, the good old times, hammered and beaten by the boots of a memorable infantry.

In the past, the beginner's course that opened the door to the barracks was held by the defaced wall of Rue Saint-Vincent, where Roger's gang brought together the many different facets of its being. Depending on what time it was, the past struck me as cheerful, comical, or quite simply sad.

Without having to force my memory, I could see, on a screen darker than ebony within the walls of my room, the gang's lugubrious procession through the fairly sinister beginnings of a poverty that would become all too familiar. Thin, imponderable shadows made their way, their feet battered by the uncaring cobblestones, toward goals that were often piteous. It was difficult to locate one's lucky star when the sun was shining. Furthermore, we preferred the nighttime, that accomplice of clothing worn through to the lining, if we were to smile a bit about our fortunes. Some drank themselves to death; others were broken by the police. Yet others became good husbands, and thereafter, decent fathers and family men. Very few left a name on the frontispiece of a book or in the bottom corner of a quality canvas. I was thinking, of course, of the companions of the old gangs of Montmartre, around 1901. It was almost aloud that I spoke the following words in the silence of my hotel room: "And I no longer know a soul who can give me a first-hand account."

I had no idea how wrong I was.

In the morning, after my bout of insomnia, I made my way downstairs, unshaven and somewhat pale, to the office of that hotel, the name of which I did not yet know.

A large pear-shaped man was speaking on the telephone with his back to me. His pants were of gray cloth; his suspenders dangled loosely to the seat of his pants, which hung down nearly to his knees. He was somewhat comparable to a trained but neglected elephant.

The thought that I was in the presence of an aged Père Barbançon brought a grimace to my lips. The man turned: it was not Père Barbançon. He looked a great deal like him, but seemed younger to me. He seemed cordial enough, wily, and little inclined to the practical customs of public morality. This furthered his resemblance to Père Barbançon. His name was Uhle, Paul Uhle. He might have been about sixty years old. Ten years younger than Père Barbançon.

II

PÈRE BARBANÇON AND PAUL UHLE

The hotel run by Mr. Paul Uhle appeared to have been built outside of time. It was not at all frequented by the enemy soldiers. Its customers were no longer a part of that era. Laboring for their daily bread determined the days or nights of the majority of them. There were few women, but they were well chosen: pleasant, fashionable ladies who were waiting for the return of the time when they could once again sing in the streets. The men dolefully wore their chosen professions on their faces. They were not at all young, and their cheeks, often unshaven, seemed to be made of the flesh of boiled fish. The girls were in no way ashen like the men, for even the most lifeless of them still had too vivid an imagination. Fear and caution subjugated them all. I was equally afraid, yet my fear was more learned than it was instinctive. Mr. Uhle was also a learned man when it came to the subject of fear. He observed everything with cruel little eyes that were often panic-stricken, the same eyes Père Barbançon had as he sat in the shadows in his shop on Brest's Quai de la Douane, back when he had met Captain Hartmann for the first time. It did not take me long to forge a certain friendship with this man about ten years my senior, whom you could browse through like the pages of an exceptional book on days when the rain flowed through your veins the same way it did into the drains. It rained that way every day. Each night, not knowing where to point my too-resonant steps, I drank wine or liquor in the company of Mr. Uhle, who had adopted me. From time to time, he would get up out of his seat to hand a returning customer

his key, an absent-minded finger smoothing his short gray beard: surely enough the same beard worn by Père Barbançon.

One night, driven by all of the force of my everyday obsession with Uhle–Barbançon, I was unable to resist any longer and the words came tumbling from my mouth in spite of myself. I did not hear them straight away, but the abrupt transformation of Mr. Uhle's face announced the sound.

It wasn't complicated! I had simply said, "Mister Uhle, you remind me a great deal of a man I once knew, a man called Barbançon. Père Barbançon, to be exact . . ."

"Père Barbançon, Père Barbançon . . . So you knew him too, did you?"

"I heard tell of him, from an adventurer who is likely dead by now. He was known as Captain Hartmann. It was Hartmann who told me of Père Barbançon, on a night much like this one, while we drank in an accursed but rather well-known port."

Mr. Uhle did not answer right away. He moved very slowly toward a cupboard that was craftily hidden by the floral wallpaper. The cupboard contained several bottles and a number of automatic pistols. I had just enough time to catch a glimpse of the contents. Mr. Uhle was trusting. He set a bottle of cognac down on the table and filled our glasses.

All of the hotel's customers had already returned for the evening. In the night, we could hear the sound of an automobile as it laboriously climbed Rue Lepic.

"Père Barbançon is surely dead by now?" I asked, in order to break the silence.

"He is dead," said Mr. Uhle, stroking his beard. Then, staring at me quite suddenly, "You must understand, Monsieur Nicolas, that it's an incredible coincidence for me to find, here in this tackle box without lures, a man for whom the name Père Barbançon elicits anything more than a decent one-liner."

I laid all my cards on the table.

"Signorina Bambù, the Océanic Bar, Joan Labet . . . and sweet little Lia who lived on Rue Peter . . ."

"Well I'll be damned . . ." said Mr. Uhle. "You seem to know a fair bit about the subject."

Our conversation was interrupted by the front bell, and so frenzied was its ringing that we both leapt to our feet in unison. Mr. Uhle having pushed the button, the door opened and the shadow of a man slipped in and out of sight, a tremendously flat silhouette. The man very quietly closed the door. He listened a moment, trying to make something out in the silence of the street. He came toward us without a sound, for he wore espadrilles in spite of the rain. He was young, slightly wild-looking, and his breathing was erratic like that of someone who had been running at top speed without any particular training for it.

"Have you a room for the night?"

Mr. Uhle looked him over carefully, taking his time.

"I haven't got a room, everything is occupied . . . But rest assured, you will still sleep here tonight."

The young man managed a bit of a smile.

"Here, drink this . . . This will put things back where they should be," said Mr. Uhle, filling a small glass with cognac.

"I've got money," said the young man as he drank.

"That is of little importance," replied Mr. Uhle. "You can sleep here, in the night porter's bed, he is away a few days. After that . . . well, that is of little importance as well. Only tonight matters to you."

"You seem like a good fellow," said the stranger. "Top me up if you don't mind." He threw a few bills on the table. "A round on me."

Mr. Uhle filled the glasses. And the man seemed to relax. His expression gradually opened up. "I thought I was being followed . . . And I *was* being followed. And so, I ran, oh how I ran . . ."

The memory of this made him laugh until he was in tears.

"Listen . . ."

Mr. Uhle raised a finger. From the direction of Rue des Saules, we could hear the indistinct sound of foreign voices in the distance, then the heavy pounding of boots on the cobblestones.

"Quickly, get undressed," said Mr. Uhle, "and get into the bed in the hallway; the bed is under the staircase . . . Yes, that's the one."

I helped Mr. Uhle ready the cot. In no time at all, the man had climbed into bed fully clothed, but having first dressed himself in a blue canvas smock and a black and yellow striped vest.

"Don't forget, your name is Jules . . . Jules Bile, my night porter. I have your papers. Don't speak too much. Everything will be fine if we remain calm."

We went back into the office so as to be farther away from the street, from the night and the heavy silence that had once again asserted itself. But the night was full of lights and noises that came and went: ancient lights shut away in people's libraries and familiar noises left over from the earliest ages of humanity, from before our mother's first birth pangs.

"There are iguanodons roaming the streets," said Mr. Uhle. "They have abandoned the swamplands and the sooty clouds, the too-yellow sun from the birth of this egg we live on. It is this hereditary fear that gives men and children alike the night sickness. Every night I am stricken; I descend into myself as one would into a cellar, and God knows what always blows out the little stub of candle that was meant to guide my steps. There I remain, as if frozen, no weapon in my hands in a world brimming with age-old moaning. It's elevation into the depths, if I might put it so."

"I'm going to go to bed," I said in reply.

"Oh, hell! Wait with me a little longer. The man is asleep. Tomorrow he will continue on his way. Don't leave me alone."

He poured me another drink.

"I would prefer to have someone with me if . . . if they come. I don't think they will. They would already be here by now. The walls surrounding the Place du Tertre must have kept any sign of this adventure to themselves."

He listened once more, very attentively. Then he went over to the young man, who was sleeping deeply, curled up in a ball. He looked him over benevolently.

"He looks a decent sort," he said. "A kind Breton face, the face of an honest man . . . I suppose you can guess what happened?"

"Can there be any doubt about it?"

"And yet, the elements of a tragedy are always the same: night, dawn, fog, the two twilights, silence, and the little bell of the Sorbonne, the one

Villon wrote about. If I were a writer, I would write a book called *A Compendium of Warning Signs*, based on the influence of those many elements; nothing could be more of a classic . . ."

It was dawn. I unhooked my key from the board. A few moments later, I was in my bed, surrounded by all of the romantic accessories that led up to the fall of the house of Mr. Roderick Usher. That tale had always had a power over me for reasons I cannot properly define. It was simply an obsession with a particular atmosphere from whose sinister attraction I had found it difficult to break free. I fed that tale with my own substance, as if it were an incurable illness. Might Mr. Uhle know something further about the destruction of that perfidious country house, imported from abroad? As I fell asleep, I blended the landscape of Usher with Mr. Uhle's dawns and the nights of Père Barbançon.

III

THE ORIGINS OF THE BOARDING HOUSE OF USHER

Five years to the day after that trying night, Mr. Uhle told me his own story and how it was mixed up with those of Captain Hartmann and Père Barbançon. Well, more particularly with that of Père Barbançon. My role in this narration will be limited to the odd polite interjection and occasional comments for my own personal use.

Mr. Uhle possessed all the qualities of the perfect storyteller: he was slow and prudent. He knew how to modulate the tone of his voice in such a way as to astutely dissemble his thoughts, which always remained somewhat hidden. Were he to say, "When you come right down to it, Père Barbançon was a dog," he would accompany this disrespectful statement with such a grin that the listener would remain convinced that Père Barbançon, far from being a deplorable individual, had all the same qualities as the best of men. For this reason, Mr. Uhle's account pleased me a great deal, because I prefer to not know the true thoughts of the people with whom I spend my time. From this moment forward, then, I will give the floor, as they say, to the honorable Uhle, who consequently assumes any and all responsibility for his own fabrications and observations.

"I knew Père Barbançon," said Mr. Uhle, "back in Rouen, on Rue des Charrettes. I believe it was 1901. You might even have crossed paths with him, as you were also a regular in those parts. Now that I think of it, I doubt he was still in Rouen when you arrived in that city, which was at that time quite an amazing place for vagabonds of fortune. If I refer to them as vagabonds of

fortune, it is to better indicate that you were not truly vagabonds, destined to vagabondage in the same way others are bound to whatever profession it is that puts food on their table. I felt a very genuine feeling of sympathy for vagabonds; I appreciate them as a social order, much as I do all disciplines that involve a certain amount of funambulism.

"I have never written anything because I have spent enough time telling my stories and problems to everyone. In telling them, it's almost as if I had written twenty books, a hundred novels, and ten thousand newspaper articles. Talk isn't published, and that is truly unfortunate, for by now the name Uhle would surely be famous."

With a modest smile, he added, "A little bit famous."

Then he went on with his tale.

"It was around that time, when I was involved with the organization of the Brotherhood of the Pan, which more specifically represents the vagabonds of the street, that I was first taken in hand by Père Barbançon. Among ourselves, we referred to him as Snark, likely in homage to the Lewis Carroll poem.

"Snark ran a bar patronized by sailors from the north, those from the forests of Norway, and officers from the few colliers that were regularly moored around the quays of Rouen. I will not bother telling you about that bar. Perhaps you have heard of the Criterion? Before you arrived unfettered in the port of Rouen, the Criterion was kept by Père Barbançon; it was fifteen years before the last infantry war.

"I started as an errand boy in that establishment, which is to say as dishwasher, page, porter, and doer of Important Deeds. To this I will add that the barmaid was a certain Miss Barclay, Annah Barclay, born, as you might expect, in London. She had a friend in Rouen who was employed by a shipbroker. Miss Barclay never enters into our game. We will leave her out of the story, if it is all the same to you.

"I will cover this period of our lives rather quickly, that of Mr. Snark as well as my own. Younger than he, I fell prey to his influence. It was he who made me the way I am today, by which I mean a man with little in the way of human value. I was nevertheless able to defend myself against the dangerous corruption of that infernal poet of dishonesty. I praise the heavens each and every time I draw a breath, my conscience as fresh as a clean, well-ironed handkerchief. I was honest the same way some people are born with blond or brown hair, meaning I didn't have to worry too much about the many prejudices that hinder the lives of such reprobates. Now that Snark—I mean Père Barbançon—is no longer, I believe that he was not quite as nasty or as vile as those who knew him in his public role may have thought. Père Barbançon was born with a double who hadn't fallen nearly as far. But Père Barbançon's good side belonged to the realm of literature. This was not the man from his own books. When he took possession of the house of Mr. Usher, far off in Brittany, in the moors that had become home to V-2s that had run out of steam, he wrote poetry, because that bandit of the highways and byways was well acquainted with fear. It was fear that made a poet of him, at least in that it offered him a turn of phrase that was easily set to music. He was the author of *The Java of the Lemures*, which was a great success at private get-togethers.

"And so I will begin my little chronicle of the contemplative life of Père Barbançon, starting around the time he purchased the famous home of Casimir Usher—doubtless a descendant of Roderick Usher—in the remote wilds of Brittany, between the barren sea and the isolating moors. In those days, that adventurer from Barcelona, Brest, and the docks of London, and I believe from Hamburg, had decidedly had enough of all that business of automatic pistols, secret languages, and young women who were the farthest thing from relaxing. In a word, he was disgusted with the business of espionage, which he had practiced for a long time, and to the detriment of that wonderful Hartmann. Hartmann, of course, had died more or less honorably in the supreme chaos of an aerial bombardment, on foot, in a tweed suit and a dirty shirt, on a road in the south.

"I was never mixed up with his shady business, and I never knew for which power he was working. If you ask me, he simply played at espionage on behalf of the Devil, and hoped to find a prominent position in the kingdom of that fallen angel. He didn't feel certain enough of his prospects of finding a job in Heaven, a Heaven of gold and periwinkle blue.

"We left Rouen in . . ."

Mr. Uhle searched for a small notepad in his pockets, but in the end he failed to locate it.

"I have no idea where I've put it. It is of little importance. We live in a time when dates, to me, seem uncertain. For example, I can no longer tell yesterday from next Tuesday. On the other hand, Christmas Eve, which we have only celebrated a few days ago, to me already seems to have played out like a film I will only ever see again by chance. All of this to tell you that the funereal adventure of Père Barbançon in his desolate Boarding House of Usher could belong to the future just as well as the past. This technique is excellent; I make use of it for my every spiritual requirement . . . I am aware, however, that sooner or later this method will play a dirty little trick on me, as they say. There are nights when I feel like death will never catch up to me. I do not fear death, as right now I am living, if I might put it this way, in a time that allows me to think that I died in 1939, or perhaps in 1655 in the days of the plague in London, which for me has always been an event that I force myself to commemorate with appropriate reading. We do not die twice. Writers die twice, but their second death is called Being Forgotten. Tomorrow, I will describe for you the Boarding House of Usher and its clientele, the memory of which often disheartens the hotelier I have since become."

IV

SNARK-BARBANÇON

Tomorrow is a modest future, the resolution of which seems to be lethal to many optimists. The confidence many men have in that word tends to hold up against all of the fuss of those who quibble about everyday life.

Mr. Uhle believed in that word. And he had reason to, for the day came when he was once again able to locate the famous misplaced notebook in its usual place, the inside pocket of his smoking jacket.

I was not indifferent to his delight. My curiosity had been awakened by the time Mr. Uhle had spent in Rouen, the city where I myself had acquired the rudiments of a literature which was often filled with the language of the streets, but always subject to sentimental acquisitions of a most permanent merit.

To me, one fact seemed beyond contention: Uhle had swum in the dirty waters of the gutter, in those small, since-lost streets which led to the wooden freighters from Norway, across from Petite Provence.

Age had already begun to cloud the clarity of the photographs that had been recorded by my memory. A charming confusion held sway over my recollections: the names of people who had been drunk on delicious humility blended with names that were under copyright and forged in printer's ink. Conrad, Captain Bannister, the Nordic painters, Lord Jim, Fultah Fisher, Mulvaney, my brother Jean, Paul Lenglois, Mr. Altmayer, the young ladies of the Criterion, the Albion, and the truly distinguished little cafés, had become informally woven together into a very fertile collaboration between the dead and the living.

Despite the fidelity of my memory, as I foraged through nocturnal enumerations I was unable to put Mr. Uhle in his place, or, to put it more simply, into the shape of a living being. Uhle was the living dead. He was, I am pretty much sure, a cross between an enumeration of juvenile experiences and a table of contents full of stillborn poems.

"A duck digging through scant refuse with its bill, that is what I am, or at least that is a side of my personality at rest," Uhle would often say when his critical side was keeping him in check.

Without accepting this definition, it was still easy for me to grant him my approbation, even more so because while he stimulated my curiosity, Mr. Uhle also contributed, with his flowing speech, to providing me with a moderately good mental image of relaxation in a well-heated room. Uhle's diction maintained a temperature between sixty-one and sixty-eight degrees, regardless of the fuel he used to feed it. Although he often set his literary landscapes in the vicinity of Surabaya, our conversations never reached tropical temperatures. Uhle was a creator of vacuum-sealed typhoons, muffled storms, and half-hearted explosions.

The discovery of his legendary notebook, held closed by a frayed elastic, set him atop a slope he enjoyed, a long slide toward his past which I found interesting. However, the many portals of my own memory were closed to the mysterious circumstances that had placed me within the scenery of his tale.

From his very inconsistency, Uhle extricated a marmoreal solidity. As soon as he had located the date of his departure from Rouen, I was abruptly caught up in the smells of the city and the comfortable sensation of warm rain on my shoulders, which were once again sensitive beneath the mediocre protection of an old jacket of English wool decorated with a belt of the same material. That had been one of my greatest desires back in 1902. That old greenish jacket with its brown checks rejoined within its moth-eaten memory the many forms of Uhle and, even more so, of Père Barbançon, that egg lightly covered in gray down, who seems to me to have been the true driving force behind this sentimental chronicle.

If Mr. Uhle still remains a poorly defined worm for me, a larva crammed full of undesirable foodstuffs, the same cannot be said as far as

Père Barbançon is concerned. Or at least not the way he was in those days: head like a duck egg, warmed by drink in Petite Provence or other places of ill repute that were haunted by the morality police, his men-at-arms and his ladies in waiting.

On the corner of Rue de la Vicomté, not far from the little door leading to that small bar they called La Parisienne, there stood a white marker, a nocturnal marker, without any discernible details, and that was Père Barbançon, scrutinizing the midnight shadows. In that darkness, his feline eyes saw what the rest of us could not. And to us, he seemed a liar. Perhaps he was telling the truth. Even Uhle himself, his manservant and lackey, could not confirm or deny anything. Père Barbançon possessed the ability to muddle people's memories. He alone knew the secret of the diabolical soup he concocted, simmering a broth out of our grievances and aspirations.

My friends and I held our meetings in Luisa Lewis's little café. This was a bar frequented by English long-haul captains; a few French merchant lieutenants would find us there upon their return from Morocco, or Saaremaa in the Baltic. Père Barbançon wasn't a regular at the Albion. He was worried about running into people. "Every time I have the misfortune to run into my past, I wind up with a lump on my forehead," he would say with an amiable smile, as if to offer his apologies to that same past. In a gesture of futility, I question myself about the presence, in my own life, of this fog in human form. And yet I know that he lives on, in spite of his definitive disappearance; as for Uhle, whom I can reach out and touch with my hand, I am certain neither of his temporal presence, nor of his social consistency.

The final image of Père Barbançon conserved by my memory, from an era completely unknown to the aforementioned Uhle, is of him as he wormed his way down Rue Grand-Pont toward Rue Saint-Etienne-des-Tonneliers. That old black-market Edward the Seventh (in contraband, as he looked a great deal like the English king) wore a black alpaca jacket and gray cottonade pants. Bare-headed in spite of the sharp cold, he sauntered nonchalantly, singing to himself in a feeble, provoking tone. In his hand, he held a short and heavy iron bar wrapped in thin colored paper, the kind the confectioners use to decorate the apple sugar so popular in Rouen. The whole was completed by two ribbons of periwinkle-blue silk which held the rolled-up paper in place. Père Barbançon's name for that toy: his "Silencer." It was most likely a few years after Captain Hartmann's adventure in the London night: that business with the Colt. At the same time that Barbançon, in the employ of the police, held sway over the sometimes secretive twilights of the streets of Rouen, I was preparing to take my leave of that city. I still have, from those days, a melancholy song that I had written on the second floor of the Albion, in a room where the parquet floor warped up each time it was washed. Tilly served as barmaid; she came, she told us, from Ireland. She served the customers, always dressed in black, her neck framed by a starched false collar. When she was serving, she wore a small white bib apron. The spitting image of one of Lautrec's barmaids, like those from Le Havre around that same time.

Here is Tilly's song. Its melody is mournful. Hundreds of songs were written to this same tune around 1900 or 1902.

SONG FOR THE BARMAID OF THE "CRITERION"

When first I found you down by the Seine Almighty
Drunk on life, dark of hair, your curves quite generous
Among carp and barbels, you were Amphitrite
You preferred your herrings be youthful and jealous.
For them you'd don your rags, fresh back from the mender;
And each night earned your way with a wink and a smirk
But you were, my dearest, too dreamy and tender
An old-fashioned romantic in love with her work.

To the Criterion Bar when coins you did miss
Barmaid for the sailors from north of the border
The boys from the freighters they all called you their sis
Ten bob for your coin purse in pretty short order
After all that business 'long the Port of Shadows
And then on Rue Grand-Pont, 'twas that Chabonnais guy.
Oh how you suffered 'til those days came to a close
In your fake white collar it's all sun and blue sky.

I had gone out to find you in the pale, pale light
A tobacco-less morn nothing left of our pay.
We went home to slumber, guts a-rumble since night,
To our lone furnished room on Rue des Cordeliers.
And oh how you could sleep, as if still just a girl
Across your half-open mouth a smile slowly crept
Life's most filled with beauty when 'neath a quilt you do curl.
The prize flow'r of the bunch for our mem'ries is kept.

When I left our Rouen and its joy-filled soirees
To toil away at the Mourmelon encampment
Farewell did I bid you, turning to hide my gaze
Yet quite softly you gave me your nod of consent.
We were sure it would be the war to end all war
At Bar Nielsen near the clock, inebriated
That one, he's a cop, a role we cannot ignore
Your tab, say your thanks, has been exonerated.

That song, stripped of its sorrowful tune, is a perfect example of what made up the literary climate that drew its inspiration from Père Barbançon, and later from Mr. Uhle, that hotelier whose wrinkled skin brought to mind a palimpsest.

The era conjured up by Mr. Uhle, when he himself entered into Père Barbançon's sphere of influence, was situated around the turn of the century, or to be exact, right around 1901, the year Uhle became fused to the destiny of Père Barbançon. This was around the time my own initial studies were preparing me for the sentimentality of the military camps, which was to follow that of the streets.

I never knew this man of ours by the name Père Barbançon. In the gang in which I was nothing more than a fragile ornament, we referred to him as Snark. It is interesting that Uhle doesn't fail to mention that name. Snark was a decidedly excellent alias. That stout man, of a strength which was quite uncommon yet which lay craftily concealed behind senile weaknesses and much squawking and griping, was easy to accept as a Lewis

Carroll character. He was born an illusionist and a conjuror. He was a juggler of lies, he ordered the most spineless among us about, and he wallowed cynically in his rumored sexual impotence, which placed him out of the reach of women, and accordingly left him safe from their gentler machinations. The girls of the street feared him as a bronchitic would a draft. And yet, he would gallantly offer them his arm to cross the street on those days when the cops would blow in and sweep the sidewalks, forcing the women to make a run for it, knees high and curses on their lips.

Barbançon-Snark was at one with the wind. His tremendous yet inconsistent strength removed any question of a slap reaching the gray down of his cheeks. In our eyes, he represented old age in its least respectable incarnation. One spring day, we dropped him off on a deserted island in the Seine across from Saint-Adrien. He spent his afternoon trying to flag down "eights" who were out doing training exercises, until the lifeboat from a hopper barge ferried him up to Île Lacroix, leaving him behind the Folies Bergère. That evening, he came to find us at the Albion. He was white with muted rage, but still affectionate. When generosity beamed forth from his face, the weakest among us groped for the butts of our revolvers. You never know . . .

Mr. Uhle had a recollection of Snark which was not at all the same as our own. Uhle, a poet in the vein of Lautréamont, attempted to rearrange the aesthetic appearance of his everyday life. He did not lie. Rather, he recounted the experiences of his own truth, which was neither our social truth nor that of our best-hidden secrets. I didn't know quite how to translate it, the same way I never quite figured out how to translate Snark's personality. In short, I was an honest man who was not self-aware.

I find Uhle's story, and that of Barbançon, to be more profoundly touching than that of Captain Hartmann, who was nothing more than an offshoot from the liaison of those two trees.

I only knew Hartmann through the intermediary that was Hamburg. Without the presence of the Reeperbahn, Hartmann simply would not exist. Uhle, on the other hand, now he was a night when fear rode through the streets; Barbançon-Snark was fear as well, but rather that congenital fear that makes infants cry for unknown reasons. Which, in my opinion, must be related to an instinctive premonition regarding the future of the world we live in.

Later on I will tell you what I know of Uhle, much as in the first part of my tale I told what I knew of Captain Hartmann after his confession in the smoking room of that very distinguished hotel. For the moment, it is Père Barbançon who has come back to torment me once again in the more human form of Snark. It was not until much later in the chronology of my reflections that I was able to make out his similarity to a child's red balloon; his behavior was that of an imperishable hot-air balloon, he had a disturbing grace which reminded me of an eggshell dancing atop the water jet of a carnival fountain.

In Rouen, our Snark lived from hand to mouth and from night to day. The loftiest of creative visions always overshadowed the numerous daily dishonesties that allowed him to eat his modest meals in a small restaurant on Rue Saint-Romain. Occasionally he would invite me to his table, not out of sympathy but driven by the need to teach. Snark-Barbançon's conversation was in no way picturesque. He could speak eloquently on a variety of subjects, the list of which ranged from the breeding of the Papillon rabbit in Florida to the possibilities of sodium bicarbonate blended with cider. He reserved his infinitely varied assortment of inventions and amusing knowledge for his own solitary meditations. For a period of several months, our opinion of Snark hardly varied at all, and we would have summed him up as follows: Snark, as God made him, was the King of Liars. Then, it just so happened that a fortuitous occasion came to modify that overly certain assessment. To our incredulity, we learned that Snark, with his own revolver, had shattered twelve consecutive empty eggshells as they danced atop a fountain; he had conversed, inside the enclosure of a large, touring circus, with a group of American Indians, and *in their language*; he had been recognized in Salles's bar by a long-haul captain who had circled the globe three times with the sole intention of kicking his teeth in. All that ended up coming of it, during the ensuing encounter, was that the captain had voluntarily shelled out for an evening's worth of libations. After a number of drinks, a former Haitian consul from Norway with a knowing look, a man who clearly didn't want to reveal all he knew to the likes of us, had seemed

shocked to learn that Snark had not in fact been hanged as he had clearly deserved back in 1897.

All of this had the terrible smell of classic truth. And yet our nights were brought alive by those surprising stories. Snark took root in us like pigweed, like couch grass. He bloomed in all seasons, and his flowers were paper flowers good enough for a printing press.

There are men still living who would be able to vouch for the lofty sincerity of my testimony. I am thinking of Paul Lenglois, or of Edouard Hibou back when he won the middle-distance track championship by hugging the corners of the velodrome in Rouen. Snark showed great contempt for sport; he considered it to be a diversion for elementary school students, good only for creating a bit of ephemeral tranquility in the closed world of schoolchildren.

Since that time, he has never stopped prancing up the old roads and down the most modern of streets, using the name Père Barbançon. When did he take up that name? If I am to believe Mr. Uhle, it was after he took his leave of Rouen. He knew Signorina Bambù, this much is certain. He must have crossed paths with her once again in London, before she bowed down to the decisive impact of the correctional fusillade.

So very many people of such diverse character were companions of Père Barbançon that it is necessary to embrace Captain Hartmann's tales as truth. I will not say as much for Mr. Uhle, whose character seems more complicated to me. I would leave to you the pains of discovering it, at the moment when he first entered the Boarding House of Usher, if, for my own peace of mind, I did not feel the need to plant him more concretely on his own two very human feet.

To truly know a poet, you must have seen him eat.

Père Barbançon was a drawing by Bofa. I know I can always find him in that form, and this aids me in condemning his acts. When I struggle with Père Barbançon, I am struggling against a Bofa character, a secret idea composed of flesh and blood, more vulnerable still because of his humanity than anything of personal interest brought on by the Apocalypse.

Seeing as songs have a great influence on the unfolding of my days, I find it difficult not to write down the Song of the Snark. By doing so, I will have wiped away all my direct connections to this indiscreet obsession.

SNARK'S SONG

In his moth-eaten hide
Of romantic alpaca
Mister Uhle's watched by Snark
In the before-dawn dark
Vignon, vignette, and viragon.

Snark belongs to Rouen
Much like that warring maid
'Bout whom much has been said
In fertile times now gone
Vignon, vignette, and viragon.

The nights he did unfold
Like films of conjecture
Tales for us he begat
Pretty cats dead and cold.
Less man, more bearded rat
Eyes like forget-me-nots
A foul-smelling python.
Vignon, vignette, and viragon.

As J. Snark we did know
Him in lit'rary days
From a most humble start
False archer with no bow.
Called me Pierre in cafés
Pierre it was, whereupon . . .
Vignon, vignette, and viragon.

Snark I have laid to rest
Thirty years paid my dues
This ballad has been drawn
From his gay sense of jest
Ode to the Pantheon
The bleakest of values.
Vignon, vignette, and viragon.

V

MR. UHLE UP CLOSE AND PERSONAL

As I describe Barbançon for you, making use of my memories of Mr. Snark, I will quite naturally include Mr. Uhle, with his lymphatic flesh like crab-meat and his tortuous, third-rate soul. With Mr. Uhle, the good was in his way of conceptualizing social morality. He was certainly less destructive than Snark. All the same, he was an unconscious destroyer of red blood cells. As you are aware, I had known him on the heights of the butte Mont-martre, where the wind that had shaken Beatrice's celestial rose gave way to creeping drafts. For the wind that gusted through Place J. B. Clément did nothing to evoke the perished house of Emily Brontë. Instead, it preferred to send swaying those somewhat mystifying elements of a joy forged of lo-cal interest.

But the night I met Uhle in the lounge of his hotel, facing the harm-ful effects of an exceptional dawn and the absence of his night porter, that night contained a new chapter in the story of fear. Uhle and I, we both knew it but we bit our tongues even as we shielded the Breton from the enemy's pursuit. Mr. Uhle's manner had given me confidence. In spite of everything I now know of him, that still speaks in his favor. That, perhaps, will be of service to him one day or another.

As you read the rest of this chronicle devoted to the comings and go-ings of the Boarding House of Usher, you will discover with sadness that this flunky to the ghosts of furnished hotels was nothing more than a po-etic aspect of the street, and yet a poorly born aspect, poorly instructed and misshapen, a distorted element of the poetry of the working class, drunk on the uncouth poison that is fear, and of all the lechery which derives from its power. Before entering into the service of Encolpius, Grimaut, and Klinius, he had learned the art of the glass-washer as early as his premature departure from high school at sixteen. From that period in Mr. Uhle's life nothing is known, other than the fact that he was caught by his employer, a man from the Périgord who never kept anything to himself, as he silently admired the backside of a young serving girl squatting down to relieve herself. The Périgorder looked over the observer as he hid behind a tree. He shook his hussar-of-Rattky head and repeated the gesture made by the Baron of Thunder-ten-tronckh during one of young Candide's more serious exploits. Ever since that day, Uhle had remained wary around women and always kept silent when it came to romantic preoccupations. Before the sojourn in the Boarding House of Usher was to transform him once and for all into a sweetbread dressed in steel-gray twill, he spoke flippantly of women. He would say, when he felt a strong need to confide in someone, "She's a little tramp . . ." or even, "She's worth about as much as mining rights in La Bamboula." The four or five phrases that made up the expression of his thoughts established his reputation as a level-headed man. His colleagues would sometimes call upon him to fill in the boxes of their tax returns. One year, I called on his expertise and entrusted him with several fiscal problems to resolve. I had some headaches. Uhle's head for business was actually quite astute. That underdeveloped character was a genius when it came to all things rudimentary, and he had a taste for imperfection. He sometimes gave the impression of someone who had dressed up in tails for the soirée but had forgotten to pull on his pants. With my eyes closed, I can do my best to reconstruct him. My hand draws him on the page; I glance at the rough outline. There is always something missing from the portrait. I have never succeeded in completely reconstituting Mr. Uhle's face; someone has always run off with an eye, the nose, an ear. Other times, I notice that Mr. Uhle has a dozen ears encircling his forehead like a garland of oak leaves. So many imperfections added to so much clandestinity of thought ought to have opened up for him the wide world of Threepenny poetry. He was a character right out of Gay's opera and his ancestors must have intermingled by marriage with the blood of Polly Peachum and Crook-Finger'd Jack.

If nature had allowed it, I would have composed an opera to be performed by Uhle, Encolpius, Diablois, and Klinius. An opera sung mutely by those voiceless and stammering tenors, an opera for those beggars of secret thoughts, illustrated by policemen's ballets and by exchanges whispered behind cupped hands.

Snark's influence on Uhle was profound and left a mark on him much in the way the executioner would brand the fleur-de-lys on the shoulder of a condemned man with his red-hot iron.

It has become difficult for me to dissociate the two men. And I think, to say it more simply, that Mr. Uhle was nothing more than a secret incarnation of Barbançon. A shared vascular engine kept them moving; a shared stomach sustained their life. Uhle was nothing but a crude materialization of the by-product of the Snarkian imagination.

It is disastrous to have to live in uninterrupted contact with the by-products of the imagination. Père Barbançon's conduct seemed logical to me: he had split into two, leaving to his double a semblance of a personality which—so he hoped—would absolve him from all responsibility for his cerebral creations.

It was while this rupture was taking place that Père Barbançon disappeared from the public eye. With a single swipe of an eraser, he had erased Signorina Bambù, Captain Hartmann, and me. Or at least he believed in the effectiveness of his swipe of the eraser. Even if he failed to completely escape the dangers of turbulent public life, he liberated himself all the same. He became lighter, more transparent: a featherweight attached to the chronicle of these past years by way of an extremely fragile piece of string.

This can help in explaining his crazy, puerile erraticism and the funambulistic ambitions he had toward that ancient and duplicitous carnival side stage, a venue for which Europe was paying quite dearly.

The readers of this book will have a good deal of difficulty piecing together the details and the climate that were in force at the end of a civilization which had been honorable in its day. Even as a new manner of intelligence was being born, vast forces of sentimentality were being lost in a completely new void. It was no longer possible to know what value ought to be attributed to emotions. And prices were collapsing. A market crash for Mimi Pinson's gold mines, Napoléon's steelworks, and the illumination of the midnight hours. One had only to consult the popularity ratings of the fashionable songs each day to be able to evaluate the mounting disaster. One had only to hear the dated, nasal voice of the market price announcer from the secondary exchange: "*Manon, voici le soleil*, down from yesterday. *Mademoiselle Clio*, down from yesterday. *Le temps des cerises*, not listed. *Auprès de ma blonde*, down. *Berceuse militaire* by Montéhus . . . ," etc.

That "etc." represented the demise of our habits of sentimentality, and the end of certain landscapes that had already been transformed by aviation and by our hopes for this recent development. All of this was set among poorly understood ideals inspired by similarly bombarded atoms. We yawned at the premise of a permanent fireworks display, and even the most sedentary, who were the most firmly secured to the ground, dreamed of new relationships, preferably of the Martian variety.

All of these reactions in face of a clear-enough future were not enough to provide me with much confidence in Père Barbançon's tendencies. Yes, even though the hour did not seem favorable to the presence of such "discombobulations," as Uhle would say. Barbançon the translucent gamboled about like a soap bubble caught in a delicate breeze, Barbançon weighed a ton in the pan of the balance scale to which I was clinging in the face of the legendary bombs of the future. The laboratory life, thanks to the gazettes, made its way into the most humble dwellings. Rumors about heavy water were replacing the traditional Sunday hen in the elementary makeup of France.

As for me, I did not believe in Henri IV's Sunday hen, but I still had faith in my past. The time had come to put a semblance of order into my losses and my gains. I had made it as far as Snark's chapter. I needed to be done with the tale of Snark once and for all, either by placing it in the profit column, or in with the losses. That is the goal that I have endeavored to attain in the chapters to follow. When I first encountered Uhle, under circumstances which I have revealed to you, the man was already too fully formed for me to be able to take his measure. He ran through my fingers like fine sand. And yet, through certain surreptitious connections, he rejoined me in the past, during the best years of my sentimental life, as it was when I knew Captain Hartmann. If I had been able to meet Uhle in those days, it is quite likely I would write entirely different things about him.

When all is said and done, there are still moments when Mr. Uhle is in harmony with the memory of my songs. I cannot conjure up my memories of him without hearing the phonograph from the Albion with its rose-colored horn. His dead voice, that of a hoarse parrot, reduces Uhle and me to a sadly common denominator. Later on, Barbançon entered into my life along with the songs of the Bersaglieri of Ventimiglia. They lived in an old fort at the city's highest point, overlooking the sea. Signorina Bambù ruffled the green feathers of their hats with a nimble hand. Perhaps, with Signorina Bambù, it was Maria de Calci who sang for the handsome young men of the "eighth," all dressed in dark blue, their short bayonets on their hips. To your health, Corporal Nino from Florence, to your youthful gaiety, Maria de Calci. At this very moment, I too am drinking: a young wine, but in a delicate glass, too delicate for me to break against the wall of this ideal cabaret to which I invite you for the very last time.

In 1906, if I had raised my glass to the health of Maria, the singer of the Bersaglieri's eighth battalion, I would have broken that cheap glass vessel. I had others left with which I could replace this victim of the solemnity of drunkards. But the Neapolitan song is smoldering beneath the ashes: it is anecdotal, just like the past.

Uhle, and I have no idea where, had become saturated in that common bitterness like a sponge. And as he did not know how to sing, his memories were secreted from his skin during his night sweats. Or so I would imagine. When he would go down to the office of his hotel to take over for his night attendant, he always seemed like he was about to sing something, an arietta that would land somewhere between *La P'tit'dam des P.T.T.* and Catullus' celebrated *Passer, deliciae meae puellae* . . . Those vague sentimental desires were conveyed by the abnormal burgeoning of his pupils, like the surprised look of a steer that finds himself in the humid tunnel of a slaughterhouse equipped with every modern comfort.

He swallowed down a cup of hot coffee into which had been dissolved all of his bygone experiences. After which, he mechanically examined his tenants' mail and said hello to me. That man, who only existed as a

human during the twilight hours, held the pages which follow completely in his power. To my surprise, he skillfully mingled his past with my own. I am unable to deny the veracity of his account, but neither can I guarantee its authenticity.

The Boarding House of Usher is not simply a product of the deformation of my own anxieties. It exists, I know this. But in what place? The landscapes left behind by the war have been poorly sanitized of their undetonated shells and bombs. The woods are all fraught with danger, and no one really knows whether a thoughtless action such as target practice on an old, empty tin of sardines might result in total annihilation.

When I knew Uhle in Montmartre, he gave me the impression of having purged himself of his past, his present, and, as far as it is reasonable to say, his future. The final delay-action bombs that menaced him went off in the halls and the basement of the Boarding House of Usher, whose guests, not wholly killed, immediately became partially tangible shadows. Shadows who were not wholly living.

I myself am surprised to undertake such precautions before penetrating the intimacy of that mediocre guesthouse. Barring the presence of Père Barbançon, and that of Uhle, the furnished hotel's maître d', I know it to be of little value. But that's precisely it; Uhle does exist, and Barbançon, still frisky and mischievous, is bounding across the cobblestones of the streets and the dirt of the vicinal by-roads.

His fortuitous arrival is the only thing that does not surprise me when it comes to this wholesale liquidation of the reserves of sentimentality, where the "castles of yore" are reclaimed by the urgent requirements of worthlessness. Before the Boarding House of Usher , under the direction of Père Barbançon, can impose its mastery over me, I feel it necessary to make note of the importance of its foundation.

The literary origins of that guesthouse are certainly suspect: it is nothing more than a coincidence between two names. The Barbançon Boarding House would have been better suited as an emblem of that dilapidated coastal inn, discouraged as it was by its own somnolence and the chronic lypemania of its occupants.

I am well acquainted with those landscapes wallpapered with the butts of smashed bottles, rusted tin cans, sneaky stinging nettles, rotting boards, and old ink-smudged envelopes. Such details cannot help but influence the growth, which does its best to adapt. An overwhelming odor of mold thrives among the décor of its walls. Barbançon and Uhle, Klinius, Grimaut, and Encolpius are naught but mold spores enlarged to a thousand times their usual size.

If you were to look at a house or a city through the lens of a giant microscope, you would get the impression that it was a bit of cheese rind observed in a specialized laboratory. The use of the microscope deforms both imagination and optimism. For those looking through the microscope, a large city can resemble a drop of pus in the same way a given word, enlarged to the utmost limit possible for magnification apparatuses, can result in an apocalyptic vision of the end of all provisional outcomes.

From the moment they were under the lens that looked down upon the Boarding House of Usher, Père Barbançon, Uhle, Klinius, Encolpius, and Grimaut became similar to common larvae, and, on occasion, to lemures made modern by circumstance.

In that desolate landscape where the chimney of the Boarding House of Usher smoked, these formerly living men, without being dead, behaved like those perpetually inchoate forms who flip-flop back and forth between life and death. Now that I have attempted to put a semblance of order into the strange tale related to me by Mr. Uhle, I can easily accept all that might have seemed implausible to me the first time I heard it. These sorts of acceptances are not without dangers. They foster doubt, a capital doubt which leads to an inescapable metaphysics. One splits into two before the mirror: there's nothing soothing about it. And then the presence of the mirror becomes superfluous. Which is when one becomes a guest of the Boarding House of Usher just like Encolpius, Grimaut, and Klinius the Sailor. At this point in time, as I reflect a bit on the ways of men my age, there is one thing I would like to know with absolute certainty: that the Boarding House of Usher has been reduced to ashes. This would spare me a great deal of anxiety. That family home for old men, the physical decay of which places it outside of the game of life, seems to me the most treacherous

of mousetraps. Can it be avoided? I would be pleased to know, and, as Captain Hartmann had toward the end of his life, I would happily ask the question, "Do you believe that a man, having more than exceeded sixty years of age, can avoid ending up next to Klinius, Encolpius, Uhle, and Grimaut in a nursing home, and naturally, not a free one?"

Can you really call it entering the realm of the eternal to become deaf and toothless, to wear the strange face of a clumsily drawn sketch?

My answer for Hartmann, when he had asked me a question that resonated with a preoccupation of mine: "You can sleep easy; it seems to me that it's all over with now." My answer wasn't only referring to young Lia.

It might be preferable not to insist on too distinct an answer to a question I am asking during a moment of dangerous curiosity.

The discreet assistance I may appear to be soliciting seems to me in no way inappropriate. After having come to know Mr. Uhle's tale, I find myself less inclined to take him lightly. To me, he seems deplorable, for the elements of gaiety I thought I had discovered there are nothing but bits of fat baiting the spring of a meticulously odious trap. A man who wears his tale in the lines on his face can never know the benefits of solitude. The solitary Mr. Uhle could not escape the curiosity of his customers. The questions he was asked, even the most banal, became indiscreet the moment they reached his ears.

Most people thought him timid. In truth, he was vain and vindictive, but all of that subsided in the confusion of incidents that came to pass in the Boarding House of Usher.

Many people reckoned, more simply, that Mr. Uhle effortlessly embodied the imbecile in a state of perfection. This verdict did not displease the hotelier because it afforded him peace among all of those who were just trying to make it to the next day.

The porter at the hotel told me that his boss had attempted suicide, one random day in an ordinary week, at a time when nothing gave anyone cause to anticipate his action. The act failed, Uhle turned red right up to his ears. For a week, he behaved like a rascal who had been caught with his hand in the cookie jar. Then he regained his usual pallor, that chalky complexion which informed those who were accustomed to him of the boss's good mood.

It would be difficult for me to complete this autobiographical essay without discussing the customers of the hotel managed by Mr. Uhle atop of the butte Montmartre. They were no longer those of the Boarding House of Usher by the seaside. Almost all of them came from a world colored by work, of both the licit and illicit varieties. The need to earn money left them within the same ordinary dimensions as the countless characters of Parisian life. Some of them belonged to office society and lived their lives during the day; others lived at night between Place Pigalle and Place Clichy. Most of the characters of the night had given themselves over to prostitution. Those young women, very young for the most part, were falsely liberated by liquor. They were also quite difficult to supervise, even in the more or less uncomplicated boundaries of the house rules posted in their rooms above the bell that kept them in communication with the help.

They almost always showed a lack of respect for Mr. Uhle. They would tell him that his nose was best suited for vacuuming out an anthill, and that all he lacked was a propeller at the end of it to make him look like a kite.

Uhle took his vengeance on them by adjusting in his favor the break-fast bills of these shameless vamps, the pride of the clubs of lower Montmartre. The office employees, whose rooms were vacant during the day, were for the most part deferential. They called Uhle *le patron*, or even better, *le boss*, in order to situate him within the exact climate of that era.

We were, in those last years, quite a ways from the sea and its romantic influence. Uhle, who carried within him the dreary, sensual mystery of the ocean depths, seemed nothing like the way I know him to be today, after the Boarding House of Usher enriched my collection of furnished hotels.

Of the many purely material recollections I was left with by the drawing of Mr. Uhle's shadow, all that remains is a pipe rack made of gothic plaster and imitation old oak, and this song which he often sang as he looked out on the sky over Rue des Saules. Here it is such as I made note of it. Its interest is strictly documentary and will have to suffice as a preface to the actual chronicle of the Boarding House of Usher.

Uhle and Barbançon, bound as one by a chain
Mezière sings your song, in his works you were drawn
The romance of ships on the sea raising Cain
Or the censured paean of the faridon
Daine.

Born of Barka, fish with scales bright and beautiful
Beasts with skin made of pearl
Know more clearly your needs, forever ungrateful
In the troubling light through the pane
Of that legend'ry manor's salon
Usher and his infernal faridon
Daine.

Shadows rolled up in cinematic format
Pale go-betweens from hither to yon
Between old Salamis and Morgat,
Return O my captains again
With seven or eight or ten stripes on,
In the free city port of Dondaine
Upwind from Isle Faridon
Daine.

Pull on the chain of the door to the harbor
And the flush will then babble and haw
To a rowdy uprising of sirens
Mado, Nini, and Tertullia
Cigarettes in their lips, strong and limber
Will switch off the electricity
O Uhle, Ulalume, Eulenspiegel
Open the door to the mansion 'fore dawn
Of the Faridon in Faridondaine
Of Faridondaine in Faridon
Dondaine
And
Dondon.

VI

THE CONCLAVE OF SHADOWS

"At the outset of the last war, as I have told you, Père Barbançon purchased a sort of rooming house, modest in appearance. I know nothing of the Mr. C. Usher who sold it to him. From what I understand, this Usher was in no way descended from that melancholy manor whose tragic end you already know. The end of the war was accompanied by disorienting signs. In the meantime, since that night you now know all about, I had given up my hotel. I had only recently returned to it, and this you know as well as I do, seeing as you have always been so loyal to that lodging. During the few years I was employed by Père Barbançon, as if in memory of something that remained indefinable and yet was most certainly idiotic, I had lived outside of time, outside of everything that makes up the regulatory framework of man's condition. AD 1000, 1914, 1946, 2722, or 1830, take as many numbers as you want and add them up, go ahead, that is how you will find out how old I am, give or take a few centuries. I have ingested time capsules to my saturation point. Among the most funereal, the cosmic administration and its moldy civil servants seem to irritate me the most. I will make sure to bring you more specific details when we finally have a Ministry of Lost Time, a laboratory-engineered infantry, and a navy fashioned of deluxe filigreed vellum. The three years I lived alongside Père Barbançon in the lyrical humidity of the Boarding House of Usher lie at the heart of the true youthfulness of my centuries. My vision of the world has been renewed. It has misted over my eyes. The second blind man in the Parable of the Blind, that classic Dutch landscape, well, that was me before I earned my certificate in advanced player piano. And so here we are at the crux of our subject. If Père Barbançon was the skipper of that strange commercial vessel washed up on the edge of a moor among the vestiges of atomic wreckage, I was the first mate. Père Barbançon, it must be said, was no longer the man about whom you have heard so much. He limped along among his lodgers, always looking over his shoulder like a fearful wrongdoer. But allow me to tell you a little about the guests, who provided a semblance of life to that fairly extravagant inn. We had three lodgers, all elderly men: Encolpius, Grimaut, and Klinius the Sailor. In short, three vanquished men. Encolpius was born in the discard room of the National Library; Grimaut came from the film industry, where he had practiced the profession of director. His shadow uncoiled behind him like a worn-out film reel, a film dotted with little holes left by extremely luminous worms. Of Klinius the Sailor, we knew very little, other than the fact that in his ripe old age, he was regarded as violent.

"The windows of the Boarding House of Usher's communal room opened onto a landscape without order, without reminiscences. It was like being in the presence of a triumph of nature which had remained undiscovered until that very day. An unforgettable crane with a steel arm twisted like a corkscrew implored or perhaps threatened the sky. God only knew. That antique vestige of historical calamities rose up at the edge of a landscape constructed of crumbling cement and unusable iron, red with rust; vigorous couch grass grew in tufts between the cracks of a quay built of a deathly pale cement which had been strewn about like the pieces of a puzzle. The barren sea belonged to the first days of fog and water. But at any rate, such as it was, it was the sea. Grimaut found that landscape to be photogenic: he felt that the hand of man had passed through there. As was the case with many individuals of his era, his cultural intellect took its inspiration from radio and the cinema. When he spoke the words cinema, studio, and camera, he suddenly became eloquent and prophetic.

"To tell you the truth, Père Barbançon was no longer a quality audience for a man of wit. All he could do was take aim at his shadow, and our own, with the first object he could lay a hand on. With his thin lips like those of an old sheep, he would imitate the sound of a Tommy gun in action. He made me feel sorry for him.

"Life in that retirement home was primed with a coat of infernal silence. A kind of original fear, mephitic and noxious, blended with the silence, the humidity, the marine putrefaction, the invisible seaweed that entwined itself around our legs. Our band resembled a walking club for the old and infirm. We were all weak in the legs and when we would trip over our own shadows, we were not the least bit surprised. With a limp kick, we would ward off our shadows' puckish independence. But at teatime, we were already talking about it. The guestbook of the Boarding House of Usher was a funeral register bound in calfskin. Encolpius kept it up to date. Next to the signature of Petronius, you could read a quatrain by Descartes or a rondeau by Tacitus. If we are to believe Encolpius, Plato had spent a season in that hotel. This game clearly amused Encolpius, whose nervous shadow danced under the moon to the sound of an unearthly music, which seemed to spring forth from the broken cement.

"It took me a long time to determine that the independence of our shadows could not be attributed to the presence of malady-induced fantasies. It was Père Barbançon who first drew my attention to this phenomenon. He was in the kitchen; he was doing some mending in front of the oven. He told me, 'Something is rotten in the state of Denmark.' 'And what is that?' I asked him. 'It's my shadow . . .' He turned his head and for a long while he looked at the ground behind his back. At that moment, he was definitely immobile. Suddenly, he let out a tiny little cry: 'Put your foot on it, it's moving!' I thought he was going to faint. He stood there, stiff and frozen. The shadow, on the other hand, wriggled a bit. It stretched out toward the sink. Then, telescoping itself, it returned to its master.

"Père Barbançon promptly plunked himself down onto a stepstool and passed his left hand across his jaw several times. 'That's all we needed,' he said. He finally seemed to reawaken and got back to his feet. 'No matter what, you mustn't tell Encolpius what you have seen here today.'

"Why was I not to say anything to Encolpius? I never found out. But Père Barbançon was never one to confide in others. One time, and one time

only, when he seemed more crumpled than was customary, he very demure-
ly confessed that he regretted having had Signorina Bambù shot, because
she had been truly beautiful. I never knew his role in that tale of espionage
and impropriety.

"To come back to the point, I was unpleasantly obsessed by what I had
witnessed in the kitchen. The behavior of Père Barbançon's shadow defied
reason, and was in my opinion more absurd than tragic.

"The tales of fantasy I had read were of no assistance in providing a
touch of verisimilitude to that troublesome and puerile occurrence. Which
fell, all the same, within the tastes of our civilization, created as it was by the
invention of atomic energy and other messages from the first millennium.
For me, all forms of magic are just attractions from a fairground free-for-all.
This I know too well. I've run a booth like so many others. Even so, I have
never seen human shadows hung from a display like old tires or second-
hand dresses. I had never been able to buy a shadow at the flea market. Well,
it turns out I just didn't know. Nowadays, I know I can purchase a shadow
at the former site of the fortifications of Paris. It is of little consolation.

"The story of Père Barbançon's shadow does not end with that initial
emotion. I had grown mistrustful, like the cuckoo who always sings within
five hundred yards of the place where she has laid her eggs. I had become a
kind of detective-inspector in the shadow police. Those of us in Père Barbançon's entourage were all somewhat inclined to play that role. For a few
weeks, I meticulously examined the shadows that belonged to the guests of
the Boarding House of Usher. At first they all appeared to be of good quality. There were five of them: my own, Père Barbançon's, which was highly
suspect, and the others belonging to Encolpius, Grimaut, and Klinius. The
last wasn't long in eliciting my worry: it too showed signs of independence.
It seemed fatter, if I may say so, and fleshier; it seemed to offer the sun a
slightly convex surface. I remember a day when I stubbed my toe on Klinius'
shadow, which gave me the impression of a poorly laid carpet. It was an
unpleasant sensation. It couldn't be classified as hot, or cold, or viscous.
Nothing was less manifest than that uncustomary collision.

"I had to get some air if I was going to put some order back into my
thoughts. I was wearing my moleskin hat as it was cold outside, and I

followed the path that headed toward the sea; toward what was left of a port that now looked like an enormous sugarloaf broken into pieces. A few children were playing joylessly on an enormous rusted cannon, the barrel of which, chewed up like the handle of a wooden fountain pen, pointed at the sky, proof of a long-ago firing adjustment. To my eyes, that cannon, the younger days of which were surely admirable, was nothing more than a vestige of the middle ages, at least as far as long-range firearms went. It was just about as useful as a large sixteen-pound culverin, cumbersomely bound to its wooden stand.

"At the edge of the sea, men were clearing the quays, which were lined by dead ships of which all you could see were the goods-lift masts and the occasional dented or punctured smokestack. Young girls searched among the debris for wood to burn. They stared at me insolently and began to laugh as soon as I had passed them by. They were having a royally good time at my expense. I was no longer young enough to try to be witty when it came to such encounters. I shrugged my shoulders and continued on my way. The road was rotting away beneath my feet.

"One step at a time, puffing away on my pipe stuffed with farmer's tobacco, I finally reached the center of town, which was occupied by a cathedral spread out on the ground in pieces, fragments that must have weighed a ton each. An open area was visible at the mouth of a boulevard lined by rough, jagged poles: a murder of crows was holding some kind of convention there. They had the look of insolent men, somewhat puritanical. They also had the look of colonizers, of proconsuls in mourning, of serious law students.

"My first thought was to throw a stone at them. I knew enough to stop myself in time. I was not the strongest of men. And then the dead city made me turn back. I returned to the Boarding House of Usher, where the first thing I saw was Père Barbançon, looking at the ground behind his back, twisting his head first one way, then the other, which brought a scowl to his face."

VII

A FEW PIECES OF IDENTIFICATION

"You will be wanting to ask me one question: 'But what was your role in the organization of this Boarding House of Usher?' I have an answer for you. My role was that of a jack-of-all-trades, a confidant who was given room and board. Père Barbançon could not live without a confidant, and it was necessary that this confidant be distinctly situated below his own social status. In the color spectrum of sloppiness, his confidant needed to attire himself in the palest shade, the most ambiguous, the most demoralizing. His choosing me was in no way flattering. Perhaps he was right to consider my presence behind his shadow as a comfort or a kind of protection. Everything qualified me to play the role of victim in that association of aged bandits wearied by works that were violent and nearly always dishonest. The Boarding House of Usher sheltered adventurers from outside of time, men already vanquished, from a world chock-full of delayed-action mines. They were like toothless infants, animated by anxious cries and irrevocable physical decay. All of their strength was directed toward the security of their daily pabulum. Encolpius, whom Père Barbançon often called 'the Arrogant Troubadour' or 'Cybele's nursling,' was always the greediest. He ate for no reason. He was also the lightest, but with less color than a soap bubble at the tip of a drinking straw.

"Thanks to idle gossip, of course, although all of it more or less bona fide, Père Barbançon knew plenty about the pasts of Encolpius, Grimaut, and Klinius, those three exsanguinated lowlifes. They had all lived through the sort of banditry found in the narrow and consistent world of a detective

novel. Even from a purely novelistic point of view, their withered skins were not worth a great deal. They had lived the lives of crafty small-time tradesmen, halfway between the knife and the machine gun. Encolpius had a collection of scars the color of lilacs. Grimaut, who had used his profession as a filmmaker to traffic in arms, was not much better, and as for Klinius, his soul had more heft to it than a loaded gun.

"During my more lucid hours, I pulled out my hair at the thought of that strange world made up of dangerous felt puppets whom I fed each day with a politeness as derisory as it was superficial. 'Did you sleep well, Mr. Klinius?'

"I had always lived among the junk-shop worms," continued Mr. Uhle. "I know a great deal about the felted world of puppets. Up to a certain point, and one that clearly surpasses the absurd, of this I was a victim. When I was a child, I was never able to control them. Where do they come from, where are they going? Who benefits from all this in this burlesque and spirited yet poorly articulated tribe?

"These exceptional characters were not born of the working man's good mood. They come from farther afield. Were we to round up all the fetishes of our era and bring them together on an island in the Baltic, we would be witness to a strange spectacle that could grow solemn if the climate and the rumors of Europe would permit it.

"We must reproach these idols, these founders of a new religion we might refer to as the fear of bad luck, for being relatively young, and for not having passed from one hand to another. Objects that are not passed from hand to hand are for the most part devoid of importance and bereft of life. The successive masters of these objects are the ones who instill them with secret powers, in the service of evil and in the service of good.

"When one purchases a puppet that is destined to conjure up bad luck, by which I mean to unsettle the days and nights of the person who acquires it, it must be bought used in a bric-a-brac shop, and not a shop that has already become well known.

"Neither an extravagance in pink silk acquired from a second-hand store, nor a young bride pulled from a carnival 'massacre' game thanks to the company's bankruptcy, neither of these can be compared to the

futureless representatives of Mickey's myriad and joyous family, available in three different patterns.

"The bride from *Zone*, much like the one from the 'massacre' games, would have been born around 1888, when it was customary to give crude nicknames to the beautiful dancing girls of Paris. For something that washed up in a second-hand shop on Rue Durantin, she has a particular kind of liveliness. She gleams in the shadows as if composed of living, inebriated flesh. She is wonderful for metered, rhyming poetry.

"Still other guardian lares of the same stripe are little by little taking over the corners of the libraries and their armchairs. It is no longer possible to sit down without the risk of squashing one of them. These woolen gods present themselves in manners from which literature is not excluded.

"Wonderful oddities such as curiosities from the German Old Empire, the executioner suffering from an inflammation of the cheek, the peasants of the Black Forest who have lost their little checkered handkerchiefs, the kingless madmen, the decorative negroes, the anecdotal policemen, the dapper little man from America with his gray top hat, the Scot in field dress, the verger of Warsaw, and Gus Bofa's bulldog done up in kidskin, all of them find each other in the home of the collector. The way they act, you would think they were waiting for a police raid.

"Once, long ago, on the great boulevards of Paris, I crossed paths with a corpulent, half-awake man whom a group of police officers were taking to the lockup. He was followed by an entire menagerie of his little stuffed friends. This procession, all things considered, weaved in and out between the taxis and buses with a surprising dexterity. The arrest was even less legitimate in that it was not accompanied by any music. The man was running mutely toward his fate, and all the little monsters accompanied him in silence. Those of us who were witness to the scene could hardly even hear the faint sounds of their tiny felt feet. Everyone might have thought it was nothing more than a procession of masked rats. Those were the days of masked balls where the most astonishing things could be seen among the most serious families, on the condition, of course, that you were invited. And that, well, is another matter.

"Yes," Mr. Uhle concluded with bitterness, "these puerile memories weigh less heavily when considered next to the events of the Boarding House of Usher. Encolpius would tell us, 'I was born in a small-town museum, I lived in a museum of criminals, and I will die in a museum of Occult History.' He was right in his own way. He had become a kind of arteriosclerotic puppet made of rubber.

"If, to show some benevolence, I insist on the invertebrate attribute, the 'felt' side of the Boarding House of Usher's residents, it is in order to explain their end, the edict of which was handed down during the great brawl which played a part in freeing me of their presence.

"Père Barbançon's three customers, and Barbançon the hotel boss himself, they disgusted me a little more each day. The scenery of the dead city, the touching anonymity of its few inhabitants, these contributed to lulling me to sleep within that impenetrable enchantment. All I could hope for was a perfect slip-up that would assist me in pushing those four characterless testimonies of my own disgrace toward the void.

"The absence of any women in our little kingdom did not seem at all insignificant to me. There could be no question of admitting any into our family vault. But this suppression of the feminine element was not any less deplorable for this reasoning. The subject was simply never broached. One evening, however, I encountered Mr. Grimaut in the stairs. The old man was sighing as he climbed the steps; before him, he held a small lit candle whose flame was flickering. Mr. Grimaut was protecting it in the hollow of his hand. 'This is Monique,' he said in a single breath. The puff of air promptly killed the little flame. Then Mr. Grimaut began to whimper. I left him unconsoled, his head in his hands, in the darkness of the staircase, sitting on the tenth step. Every woman's name was tantamount to remorse.

"Some days, the sun shone upon our frozen solitude. It slowly aided with the construction of a new scenery: sheds surged forth from the ground with a fragile burst of vanity. A crane, capable of lifting up the dead city, extended its long demon's arm over the stagnant sea. The guests of the Boarding House of Usher took advantage of beautiful days like those to take their shadows for a stroll out in the heath. Their mutinous presence brushed against the new growth of shrubs and flickered across the nascent

water of the wastelands. Ever since the arrival of spring, the shadows had thawed, taking on strength, authority. They behaved like puppies, but puppies who were born to bite artfully, well learned in the many professional secrets that can be acquired when biting is treated like sport.

"When Père Barbançon, Klinius, Grimaut, and Encolpius would go walking together, their four shadows would follow them, frolicking like children at the end of the school day. Sometimes they would amuse themselves by switching masters. On more than one occasion, Père Barbançon returned to the Boarding House of Usher followed by Encolpius's shadow. That was the most vicious of the five shadows, my own included. It would be the instigator of a devious yet unrelenting struggle, one which would eventually lead to the deaths of Père Barbançon and his three companions. I was most likely the first to perceive all of these parasitic schemes.

"Night having fallen, Encolpius would speak to his shadow in the same way the Emperor Hadrian would converse with the woman who occupied the fourth bed. This disorder bent our daily lives out of shape, twisting the simplest events of our very existence. Throwing a bone to a shadow is like attaching misfortune to the heels of its master.

"I ruined my health once and for all during the course of that year. I slept little. Hands under my neck, my eyes wide open, I relived the day's most insignificant happenings in minute detail, peeling away the images and words as one would peel an onion. You might say, 'Why not abandon the Boarding House of Usher to its dangerous mediocrity? Why not leave?' It was as if the place was covered in birdlime, Monsieur Nicolas; I was immersed in the glue like an ant in jam. And anyway, the end was approaching, 'like a thunderclap all the way from China, from across the bay.' Dawn crept in . . . a dawn of the classic sort, but more exactly one that brought with it a bitter and sinister day."

VIII

THE DEATH OF PÈRE BARBANÇON

"I have never fully understood the reasons and surprising phenomena that brought on the revolt of the shadows. It must be explained by estimating the lyrical value of the hours in a day and a night, then inhumanly multiplying them by the exceptional gravity of the events. The supernatural sprang forth from the deepest, swampiest strata of memory. Ten-ton iguanodons replete with their sparrows' brains climbed stupefied and vindictive to the surface of unexplored waters. They lay in wait for the signal announcing the imminent disintegration of their difficult substance. At the very least, Monsieur Nicolas, that is my opinion. It isn't a dazzlingly clear assessment, but I have nothing else better when it comes to explaining the death of Père Barbançon, as well as those of Klinius and Grimaut. On that matter, I have to inform you that Grimaut was not truly a cinematographer. He was actually a long-haul captain and his name was Diablois. 'You lied, Uhle,' you will say. Heavens yes, I have lied: it is the mist that drives me to lie. I cannot see the things that live and quack away inside the fog. And so I lie in order to simplify my connections."

Mr. Uhle pulled open the curtains, which were hiding the light of the dawn. He extinguished the electric bulb, and the pale light penetrated the room, wiping away the ludicrous images of the night's dreams, a bit at a time. Mr. Uhle sat down, as if overwhelmed. He continued speaking for a long time, his monotonous voice flowing like a small but inexhaustible water leak.

"Père Barbançon and I, the trifecta, and the shadows that followed us, we were nothing but tatters of fog, dubious rags torn from the drab linen that enshrouds the crack of dawn. Yes, Monsieur Nicolas, it is daybreak, the dawn of a memorable day that did in your friend Barbançon and the others, with the exception of your humble servant.

"But I am digressing from my subject, from the novelistic part of my subject, let me emphasize, for the entire secret of this detective story lies in the fog of a dawn I first heard tell of in *Ulalume*.

"To conclude, that day I awoke around five o'clock in the morning. I opened my window and I saw the sky in its forbidding immensity above the landscape, a scenery which I have previously described for you, and the character of which is not close to fading from my memory. My mind was jolted awake by a muffled clamor, as if from a radio program, which seemed to be coming from the dining room. Faint noises, marked but indiscernible, stood out distinctly over a background of grumbled cursing and distressed moans. I stood as still as stone, my ear grasping for information. Little by little, it began to seem as if I were hearing the sound of a brawl, of a fracas, yet a fracas between wool-stuffed sailors, or perhaps a struggle between fierce old men, a struggle without weapons or mercy. For me, it took shape in my mind as a battle between sponges drunk on water, a collision of flaccid sponges swollen with heinous humidity and intelligent cruelty.

"I made my way down the stairs in my bare feet. The door to the dining room was open. By leaning my head over the banister, I saw the spectacle whose tumult I had surmised. Père Barbançon, Klinius, and Diablois (we will allow him his true name) were rolling on the floor, their eyes bulging from their sockets. Lianas of a bluish gray were wound around their necks, their legs, and their arms in a melee which made the whole look like a spilled dish of spoiled macaroni. It also resembled a furious assault by rebellious shadows. And that was exactly what it was: the rebellious shadows were attacking their masters, inexorably Windsor-knotting themselves around their master's necks, constricting about their hearts and stomachs, tying and untying themselves for new grips, secret knots of an evident efficacy. And yet, the struggle was a long one. I did not wait for the end, for all of a sudden, it dawned on me that my own shadow had accompanied me and that all of this was a dangerous example to set for him. I returned to my room and stretched out on my bed, awaiting the end of that fantastic activity. It was all quite unexplainable. Even Peter Schlemihl didn't have such an adventure when he sold his shadow to the old man at that rather Weimarian garden party. I lit a cigarette and looked at my watch: it was seven o'clock. The weather looked promising. A nurturing warmth brought me back toward optimism a breath at a time. As for the dining room, it now appeared to be free of its many monstrous noises. In two shakes of a lamb's tail, I had packed my suitcase and descended to the ground floor. I saw what I had already imagined: Père Barbançon, Encolpius, Captain Diablois, and Mr. Klinius stretched out side by side, as white as soft French cheese, their mauve tongues hanging far out of their mouths.

"They were quite dead, the four of them. That hastened my decision. My presence in the Boarding House of Usher could do nothing but cause me the full gamut of legal difficulties. It would have been onerous for me to explain that fairly outrageous tale of shadows.

"Flight was of the essence. A literary reminiscence immediately came to me to bolster that sensible decision. 'You must set fire to the Boarding House of Usher,' counseled my good guardian angel. No sooner said than done. I had gathered into the dining room all of the flammable materials I was able to find. And very artistically, from cellar to attic, I built a tinderbox capable of discouraging the most powerful fire engines. After all this, having emptied the contents of fifty jerry cans, proof of Père Barbançon's innate proclivity for theft, I waited for night to fall so I could toss the emancipating match, which would wipe out any trace of the tragedy.

"At the stroke of midnight, I went through with my plan, and without bothering to take my suitcase with me, I reached the moor, from where I was able to admire the grand finale I had sought.

"Thus blazed the Boarding House of Usher. At dawn, nothing was left but a heap of anonymous ashes. So rest assured that there exists no magic that will be able to bring back the man that was Père Barbançon. That deplorable rogue can only rejoin his old dance-partner Captain Hartmann in oblivion. You and I both, we are rid of two compromising scoundrels. It is with pleasure that I am able to confirm this, and to me, the future seems awash with clemency. Père Barbançon and Captain Hartmann have become one with those curious personal stories which often require us to liquidate the very obsessions that make them up. Other subjects will have to suffice when it comes to nourishing the reveries of the nighttime, when each one of us, astraddle a good chair, allows the generous warmth of a summer's night to blend with his most personal thoughts."

IX

FALSE CONCLUSION

A few days after that revelation, Mr. Uhle sold his furnished hotel and disappeared from my daily routine. This caused me no grief whatsoever, as I found his presence discouraging. Curiosity alone had drawn my attention to the trifling incidents detailed in his chronicle of the Boarding House of Usher. The death of Père Barbançon and the utter destruction of his mournful abode instead announced to me the birth of a new era forged of a romantic contentment to which I greatly aspired. The certainty of being rid of both Captain Hartmann and Père Barbançon left me spry and smiling. For a few days, I was a candidate, although a passive one, for a position as an active member in an athletics society that was pleasantly equipped with drums and bugles, instruments whose usage had fallen into obsolescence in recent years. I felt rejuvenated. On the outskirts of the Forest of Halatte, I owned a small house; its construction dated back to the genesis of Sylvie. This abode gracefully occupied its place within the landscape and ended up looking more like a relic of the past than an expensively renovated authentic thatched cottage. Everything seemed peaceful in the light it gave off; the men themselves seemed appeased. I lived, passing the time like a gourmet, far from the ravings of the Barbançon–Uhle Association, and anyone within reach could revel guilelessly in my glow of good health.

Which is why I was able to offer only the feeblest resistance to the vermin from former times when they penetrated the serenity I had worked so hard to acquire, arriving in the form of a letter bearing a British stamp. The letter was written in the hand of Mr. Uhle, whose capricious handwriting I was all too familiar with.

It dragged me, hands and feet bound, back into that tenacious past. Mr. Uhle had lied to me once again. Père Barbançon was not dead. Père Barbançon still roamed the highways and lurked in the streets, offering a dram of eau de vie to the young ladies and the non-commissioned officers of the antinuclear garrison. I have copied this document for you without altering a line.

Dear Monsieur Nicolas,

I lied. Père Barbançon is alive, but I am on the verge of death myself, and green with envy over the longevity of that old snake. With God as my witness, I can assure you that this time, the events truly unfolded as I am about to tell you. But you must believe me when I tell you that before my entry into that age-old western port, I had never heard of Père Barbançon. I made his acquaintance as a guest, the last to arrive at the Boarding House of Usher.

As I have already told you, the port had the look of a gigantic box of crushed sugar cane that had been spread out in the mud. I will stick with that analogy, which pleases me a great deal. A crippled crane stretched its long, twisted arm toward a shack-dotted pathway. It was a sign. At the far end of the reach of this gesturing arm, a sprawling building, somewhat colonial in style, inexorably caught the attention of the crews of the small craft which had haphazardly drawn up alongside the length of the crumbling quay where it lay, still littered in uninteresting debris. At that hour, which was fading into the evening twilight, I was on the lookout for a hotel room and a meal, and, by mental association, for some work. Memories, quite classic in their style, floated in the salty air. Which is why I immediately noticed the sign hung from that large building, a hastily erected sign that instantly gave the building an unquestionable authority: The Boarding House of Usher. My soul, at that moment, was filled with embers, and the leaves of the few plants seemed "crispèd and sere." It was night "in the lonesome October of my most immemorial year." I could hardly believe my eyes. The Boarding House of Usher, the Boarding House of Mr. Roderick Usher. Those words, without rejuvenating me personally, rejuvenated the classic spirit of romanticism, the marble slabs of which were indistinguishable from the blocks of cement that were jutting up like petrified waves. Through the curtainless windowpanes of the estaminet, I saw a large man whose pale face was adorned by a short Florentine beard. He was rinsing glasses behind the counter of his bar. A lone customer was drinking, seated at a table near a sawdust-burning stove. I opened the door, closing it carefully behind me so as not to let out the somewhat artificial warmth, which all the same provided a feeling of safety. I approached the man by the glasses and announced my desire to room and board in his establishment.

"You must be Mr. Roderick Usher," I asked, "or one of his heirs?"

"Neither one nor the other," declared the man with the short beard. "My name is Martin Barbançon, or Captain Barbançon, if you prefer. At my place, everyone is a bit of a captain, for reasons which are strictly literary, of course. This is a guesthouse. Have you any luggage?"

Upon my negative response, Captain Martin Barbançon replied, "All the better. Baggage clutters up the rooms. The baggage we carry in our heads is the only kind that is tolerable. I carry insurance against all of the dangers to which products of the imagination might expose us."

For ten days, then, I was a guest at the Boarding House of Usher. I had struck up friendly relations with the customers of that peaceable sanctuary. It was situated outside of any violent adventure. The girls did not frequent it at all, and didn't get mixed up in its drink-focused amusement. As Captain Barbançon had rightly said, our baggage was lugged about in our heads, and wealth depended on the imagination of each one of us. Even so, that congregation of people, outwardly timid, was not the least bit comforting. Each one of them kept his fears deep inside, like the pit in a cherry. The thugs who occasionally visited the Boarding House of Usher, for a lack of other choices, came from another world, the world of outdated words, of images become obsolete and photographs in the process of decomposing. My neighbor across the landing, Captain Diablois, was as

desiccated as a dead leaf; another lodger, who was as cheerful as a palimpsest, brought Encolpius to mind. Among those of our circle, he was referred to as "the Arrogant Troubadour" without any further explanation. Nobody knew why. Captain Diablois, the Arrogant Troubadour, and Captain Barbançon would often engage in long, muttered parlays that I found rather irritating as they were too unrelated to me, although they were always courteous about it. One night, after one of these puerile exchanges, Barbançon (the Captain) asked me, somewhat awkwardly but obligingly, "You are, of course, accompanied by your shadow?"

The curious thing was, that question did not seem absurd to me. And it was with the same breezy tone that I responded. "Naturally, who do you take me for?"

"Here at the Boarding House of Roderick Usher, everyone is accompanied by his shadow." To this, he added, "Some of them are rather odd, that of Captain Diablois, for example. I don't trust that one at all."

"As for me," I replied, "I have the utmost confidence in my shadow. It has attended to me since I was born. It is as faithful as an old servant, the sort you only come across in novels whose time has already long passed."

Captain Barbançon nodded his head like a man who could go on for hours about the behavior of shadows and their masters. And we left it at that, the both of us bogged down in the doughy aesthetic of that rooming house full of single men who smelled of boiled milk and lime flower tea.

However many guests there were at the Boarding House of Usher, there were the same number of shadows, which the play of the lights accentuated more or less clearly. Winter and its foggy skies set in like a season of dead shadows. In the summer, the shadows attired themselves in new livery of an ardent violet or a luminous blue. At that time, they were remarkably agile. Their independence surpassed the limits of their vagueness. All they were lacking was the power of speech; that is what my neighbor Encolpius, or the Arrogant

Troubadour, confided in me, he being one of the more eloquent among the creaky old men who fed themselves on fearful meditations in the picturesque of that grand deboned port.

The Arrogant Troubadour was drinking a glass of milk and smoking an herbal cigarette. His shadow, mouse gray, was thrown at his feet and formed a shapeless and fairly useless stain. Little by little, I had come to imagine that our shadows were like a kind of domestic servant, extremely flattened menservants, thin layers of felt for hire. The indolence of our century had made me indulgent of many things, the hostility, or even the indifference of which I could not really explain. Thanks to numerous indiscretions, I knew that all the customers of the Boarding House of Usher were erstwhile adventurers who had been saturated in violent exploits up until the more or less complete dissolution of their former personalities. Their language, having lost its form, no longer used the jargon of their often immoral or even homicidal experiences. The colors of their lives had melted in the soft, imitation warmth of the Boarding House of Usher. Conversely, their shadows prospered. They seemed to have sucked all the energy from their masters. It didn't take a sorcerer to understand that the taste for violent behavior, which had made their masters into exceptional men pulled straight out of adventure novels, had passed into them. The shadows' owners were no longer anything more than shadows of their former selves.

The presence of the Arrogant Troubadour afforded me some certitude in regard to this phenomenon, which risked posing a threat to our restfulness, being, as we were, succulent plants and not the least bit carnivorous. In his more virile days, the Arrogant Troubadour had smuggled liquor between Nassau and a few small ports in Florida. He limped from catching the contents of a magazine between his hip and the back of his knee. His shadow limped as well, but more blithely . . .

"Keep an eye on that bitch," he said, the word surprising me as he pointed out his shadow, which seemed to crumple below him.

"One moonlit night, she will strangle me. A snake through and through—just as slippery, with the soul of a snake as well."

He sighed. "When I was her age, I was like she is now . . . because shadows don't age. Time hasn't the least hold over a shadow. In this contest, you must be thinking, we have been tragically bested."

"In the past, I used to read adventure stories," said Captain Barbançon, "and I did my best to lend substance to them by the example I set myself. Today all of that seems infantile to me. Enough, let us speak of other things . . ."

"Ah! Ah!" snickered Captain Diablois. "We are dead drunk on violent acts. If they were to squeeze me like a lemon, what would come out? Knife blows, volleys of automatic pistol fire, newfangled curse words, and the names of pretty girls. I am as full of girl's names as a calendar."

"Tell us just one," said Captain Barbançon.

Captain Diablois scrunched up his eyelids, took his forehead in both hands and remained speechless, his mouth open somewhat naïvely.

"Captain Barbançon and Encolpius," said the Arrogant Troubadour, provoking a weak, inhuman peal of laughter.

"Go and ask my shadow about that . . ." Captain Diablois finally replied, "he could be vexed!"

Through the curtainless bay windows, I could see the jetty, where stinging nettles grew in the cracked cement. In the distance, under the slate-gray backdrop of the sky, at the center of the deserted beach, a long-rusted cannon pointed its ancient barrel toward the sky. The cannon had taken on the look of an arbalest, or at the extreme limit, a Veuglaire. It was from another world, old and useless. In some ways, it was like Captain Diablois, and Encolpius, and Captain Barbançon, and most likely me, but I would rather not insist on that comparison. As a spectacle, it was lacking in appeal. I had just caught myself yawning when a familiar noise clamped shut my mouth for me: a racket,

like something I had heard long ago, the clamor of a brawl. It was coming from the garden: a well-enclosed garden, furnished with ten pear trees the shape of lyres. It was hot in my room; I had just lit the fire. I took out a cigarette, and I noticed my faint shadow, glued to the wall above the chest of drawers; the sound was provoking a series of knowing undulations in him. I had little desire to learn the origin of those noises, which definitely reminded me of the skirmishes of my youth when, a soldier, I stood overlooking Artois from atop the railroad embankment at Vimy. I knew enough already, and my sack of experiences was full, like a sack of demonetized écus. Encolpius's bitter voice rang out:

"I'll show you, you deceitful weed! You disloyal kelp! Filthy apparition!"

Without a doubt, those insults were addressed to the Arrogant Troubadour's shadow. I heard yet another rat-like cry, which did not come from a shadow. It was at that moment that Captain Barbançon, who had entered my room with feline steps, said quietly into my ear, "Encolpius is taking a royal drubbing. His own shadow is beating him black and blue."

"Captain Barbançon," I replied, "we must act, we must, to be blunt, reclaim our youth. Otherwise our shadows, well fed on all our combative tendencies, will knock us about however they please, like a pair of three-dimensional imbeciles."

I will not go into detail about the assault our two companions had to withstand from their rebellious shadows. Captain Diablois, the first of them, was strangled by his, which wrapped itself around his neck like a muffler. Encolpius was treacherously crushed against a wall by his shadow, which had become as hard as a steel plate. He sighed like a rabbit and died. Their shadows likely returned to the realm of masterless shadows, in the most picturesque havens of the metaphysical adventure.

It was then that Captain Barbançon proposed a plan of action. It was not at all in my best interests to withhold my collaboration, seeing as it didn't seem to me that my own shadow deserved to be

given the slip. This plan consisted of fleeing, of leaving the various elements of the Boarding House of Roderick Usher in our dust. We waited for a full moon so that our shadows could present themselves distinctly on the smooth surface of the road. Truth be told, they were beautiful, tall, mischievous, and amicable. They frolicked around our footsteps, playing the lovely games shadows play in the virginal light of the moon. Before we disappeared behind a cliff, we took a look behind us and, for the last time, saw the Boarding House of Usher, silent and already lost in the misty haze of its infernal conclusion.

We had exceeded the standard allotment of romantic melancholy. Captain Barbançon shrugged his shoulders and switched his little leather attaché from one hand to the other. He gave it a shake.

"Inside this bag, I have a razor, a bar of soap, and my book of accounts."

My own hands were unencumbered inside the pockets of my sheepskin jacket. It was perhaps this small detail that led me to decide it was better to cut short the farewells that threatened to drag out due to spinelessness. I held out two fingers to the captain.

"Farewell, Captain Père Barbançon."

He shook my hand and went off down the road that traced its way along the edge of the sea. After hesitating a moment, I went off in search of other friends. And I heard the reveille ring out at the barracks of the Navy Riflemen.

I walked ahead of my shadow. At a bend in the path, it leaped joyously in front of me. As I instinctively looked him over, I realized that this was not my shadow, but that of Captain Barbançon. As I had never been overly concerned about ownership, I continued on my way without attaching much importance to this misunderstanding or substitution.

This account is the most unmitigated expression of the truth. It draws to a close with my own end, which is in no way a fantastic death, but rather a death easily predicted by the manuals of practical medicine currently in use. Farewell!

UHLE

The summer that followed the reception of that absurd but troubling missive, the Sunday strollers chose the elegant valley where my home had been built as the site of their daylong exploration of pastoral delights.

I did not tend to participate in the delight of young men, young women, and their parents. The certitude that Père Barbançon was not in fact dead draped a veil of crêped gauze over the apple and cherry trees in bloom. A haze of soot clung to the lilacs that framed my doorway, erasing the most dulcet scents in the world of objects, newly sprung into flower once again.

All the same, I felt no hatred for those gay and noisy holidays. I sat down beside the road's edge, in front of my door, on a stone bench I had had placed there for my comfort. Thus stationed, I went about my days with the dignity of an old man as I tried to enshroud the outside world with the blue smoke of my tobacco. I listened indulgently to the cooing of the turtledoves and the cry of the shrike as he replied to the oriole, his personal attendant. The young people no longer tried to trip me up with poor advice. It became easy for me to arrange the weekend amblers passing by as if they were figurines behind one of the windows of my library.

On a Sunday that participates in the conclusion of this tale, I was sitting on my stone bench, convinced that I must look like Minerva's bird, a classic bird, but fashioned of terra cotta. The heat of the sun, combined with a slight breeze, very readily dragged unforgettable love songs to the front of my mind, ballads which more or less summarized my memories of youth, or at least the most tender of them. A young girl of sixteen who had been my neighbor knew all the songs. She also had a sensitivity to her, and was as true as a phonograph. A thousand records would not be enough to make up for her having grown old. I only owned a dozen, in French, English, Italian, and Castilian. They were so worn that they skipped under the needle and repeated the same phrases over and over again, like that famous, nefarious raven whose parents had given the name Nevermore.

To return to the sense of well-being I was enjoying on that beautiful June day, I can still smell, as I write these lines, the scent of the new flowers, and I can hear the customary calls of the birds of Île-de-France as they marveled over the sunlight's perfection. An old rusted tank, buried in the hawthorn bushes at a curvature in the road, served as a platform for the children, who were amusing themselves by acquiring new bruises. My nose had become as sensitive to these smells as it would have been to a Bleu d'Auvergne. I was thinking that I would be able to doze in complete safety, when shrill cries and youthful singing disturbed the pink and gold calm of the countryside. I could not see the cheerful troupe whose singing had melded with the other vague noises. But that band drew rapidly nearer. I saw them appear at the bend in the road: young girls in white dresses, of course. They were crowned with flowers, like Parisian girls often are when they spend a little time in the country. To me, they seemed drunk on the fragrance of the flowers, like honeybees dressed in white. The surprising thing was that a man walked ahead of them, a big, swarthy man, most likely their grandfather or even their great-grandfather, or Silenus all done up in the fashions of the day. In any case, it was unequivocal, the fat, very old man looked like an inflated rubber drum major. He bounced along like an extra-buoyant balloon, and he kept time for their songs by cutting through the air with a stick that still bore a few leaves. When the charming troupe passed before me, kicking up an unpleasant cloud of dust, heavens above! I was quite sure I recognized the silhouette of Père Barbançon, such as I had imagined him.

He passed by without seeing me, spinning his baton like he didn't have a care in the world, aggressively, mockingly, indestructibly. Long after, I could hear the clear voices of the little Parisiennes, voices accustomed to singing in the streets:

> *Père Barbançon, son, son, son, son . . .*
> *Stand us a drop, drop, drop, drop, drop . . .*
> *Us low-ranking men of the garrison . . .*

The regional locomotive that was to carry away that flower-adorned vaude-ville routine whistled from across the woods in the valley. Once more I heard, from the direction of the train station, a great commotion of many far-off voices. Then the locomotive gave its piping cry; a long plume of smoke climbed into the sky. I watched it attentively. Did I hope to see Père

Barbançon dancing there, charming and as light as an eggshell thrown about by a fountain? The convoy pulled away. Ever since that Sunday, it has never stopped pulling away.

X

THE DEFINITIVE END OF BARBANÇON

I have returned to the old house that I have lived in, winter and summer, for the past twenty years. I have retraced my steps. But in following that invisible path, I feel as if I am really following the perverse ghost of Père Barbançon.

It so happens that for the past few nights, a kind of angel has come to disturb my sleep. Wearing Barbançon's very shape, but as if made pure by some virtuous hand, he looks extraordinarily like one of Olaf Gulbransson's celebrated drawings. This thickset, squat little angel of whom I am the disobedient ward has no qualms about reprimanding me while, stretched out on my bed with my hands on top of the sheets, I watch the smoke of my cigarette soar off toward an unpleasant sky.

To say that I have only been aware of him for the past few nights might be a bit of an understatement. To be honest, he has been prowling around in my private life ever since my youth, during an era when I had no private life. He was simply there, like a doleful pig bladder in human form, from the day I first smoked a pipe. I had promised myself it would be a pleasurable experience. He spoiled everything to such a point that I no longer know whether the malaise to which I fell victim should be attributed to the tobacco or to the presence of that angelic balloon.

The most peaceful joys in my life were always mitigated by that decoration from a university dance from whom no power was able to set me free, as he was made out of everything that is the purest in man, by which I mean the most fragile and the least useful. He circled around me like a kind of

preventative remorse and did not vanish until the asininity was achieved. I was then free until the next time. My angel had to get back to a celestial abode about which I never had enough curiosity to inform myself. But he always came back. His voice, like a stowaway loudspeaker, mingled with my fate, the tragic qualities of which I am all too aware. He can argue, the bastard, and what's more, he is mindful of the fact that he represents the least indulgent part of me. Certain circumstances upon which it is pointless to insist lend an authority to his arguments that I cannot disregard.

"Nicolas," he says to me, "reread your books, if it isn't too much to ask of you. I did it all for you. I have maintained this saddened courage, my dear Nicolas, with the hopes of including you in my pain and confusion. I grant you that here and there, you have demonstrated a certain taste for virtue, when it is discreet. This will count in your favor. But how can you remain silent when all around you the most authentic hoodlums, transformed overnight into lambs, spend their every opportunity celebrating that same radiant virtue, the brilliance of which, in days of old, they would have gazed upon through a spyglass as transparent as the leg of a barstool. I would like, my sad, sad Nicolas, in this new concert of voices unaccustomed to singing in choirs, to hear your voice. You must understand that if you want to live, you must be an educator; educate the scam artist selling his sugar and soap, the vain man who appeals to the ladies, the egotist, as colorless as a hazelnut bouillon, the hypocrite with his curly hair, the coward with his spidery script, the lustful man with his velvet eyes, and the rest of that parade. You will need to search out a new lexicon, to find words which have not managed to make their way to those who have been your masters of the fantastic. I think I can guess your response, my poor Nicolas. You will tell me that art is not necessarily educational, and that Baudelaire, who was a great poet, was also a poor excuse for a teacher. You will tell me, perhaps, that excess in all things is a fault. That sentence pleases me, as it seems bland enough to be educational. Think about it, Nicolas, and quit your sulking. Open your mind to new horizons peopled by the neo-virtuous, the rhythm of whom you will regulate. Most importantly, don't go shouting from the rooftops that an artist, a poet, and a talented novelist are all as necessary to life, virtuous or not, as a plowman or a bricklayer; I would be forced to chastise you severely. Your notions about fantasy, be it winged, aeriform fantasy or light, charming fantasy, are most likely not proof of a bad character. They are simply ill timed and prone to slowly melting away. You are not a bad kid, Nicolas, but you reason like an old man. That intellectual necrosis upsets me. If I were in your place, I would go and dig a hole in the grass of your fenced-in yard and I would bury myself there, allowing nothing but a tuft of hair to poke out, a top-knot which would then become one with nature, savoring the breeze that gambols through weeds."

My angel sighed, floated up toward the sky and bumped his apparition of a head against the ceiling of the bedroom. He came back down straight away in order to complete his sermon, the substance of which was keeping me awake.

"Nicolas, allow me to make a small gesture. I will bring you the cowl and the ash, and the gruel of Lacedaemon inside a tuna fish can. I hope to see you again soon, livelier, or at least more alert. A bit of good will and soon you'll be writing like a budget rapporteur. Before I take my leave of you this time, I would like to entrust you with a couple of books I think might help you. Here you will find *The Decalogue of the Fools* by Caitiff, *The Ass-Licker's Sermonary* by Nada, and *The Choreography of the Dullards* by Mug. If you would also like to have an aluminum-bound copy of the legendary dictionary of the . . ."

"Leave me the hell alone," I replied to my angel. "For more than twenty minutes now you have been boring me to death with your chatter. You would have more luck sending me to get permits for interplanetary travel, which would at least allow me to meddle more actively with the economic and sentimental course of our times."

That celestial sausage's most recent apparition was definitely his last. During an evening of lucid solitude, a quiet noise transformed my bedroom. My routine anxiety was able to feed on those faint, somewhat supernatural scratching sounds. I was able to look through the door without the least bit of surprise. There was the angel, wearing some sort of heavenly pajamas, sitting on my chair in front of my worktable. He was mindlessly moving a blunt quill about in the inkwell, where the hardened ink from last May was turning to dust.

"Ah! You've come back," I said without a trace of pleasure.

He did not reply. He was content to give a little nod of his head as if it hurt him to do so.

There I was, exhausted, every bit of strength eaten up by a voyage candied in those dietary preoccupations that gave our epoch a coloration that once again, at least for the moment, was reminiscent of a bad joke. The sort you believe without really wanting to believe. But my dreams had been of a butcher wearing his little smock, who was contemplating something and scratching his head as he stood between a fatted cow and a precision postal scale.

My angel must have been thinking about economical problems in the same vein, for he turned his long, beatified pedant's face toward me so as to spit out the following two words with a liberal dose of venom:

"Bone . . . in . . ."

"What can you possibly mean, O celestial guardian, by those deceitful and venomous words? Is it my physical person that you so appreciate? Are you insinuating that even 'bone-in,' this slightly tired body, which I like just the way it is, has in some way 'lost its market value,' to borrow a line from the everyday?"

"Don't play the fool," the angel said to me, without losing his translucent solemnity. "You know full well what this is all about, seeing as not even a minute ago, you were reciting your feeding tables."

He got to his feet and walked gracefully to the door. He opened it. And immediately, right there before our eyes, nature awaited, full of trees, grass, stones, and late-arriving flowers. As far as the eye could see, it was impossible to spot anything that the economists might refer to as an "edible oil product." Everything was green, like a salad without salad dressing, or dry like tinder, or indigestible like the marble of a tomb . . .

My angel was transforming before my very eyes, not unlike Sylvie on the lush lawns of Ermenonville. He pranced about like a charming puff of smoke and smiled, grasping the dead woodenness of my unearthly hand. I thought it an appropriate time to giggle, because my bitterness had me in no mood to discuss the inevitable. That giggling did not go unnoticed. The cherub-like guardian of my moral tranquility came to a halt between two saplings which were doing a very good impression of altar candles, and, in a gentle and spellbinding voice, he gave me my money's worth.

"Nicolas, enough of your sarcastic beating around the bush. The restrictions are only merited if they are not of the mental variety. Pay close attention to what I am telling you, Nicolas, for if you don't listen to me, it will burn you before too long."

I must admit, the son of a bitch scared the heck out of me. The tone of his voice, the era we lived in, that landscape completely devoid of fatty foods, all of this together returned me to those worrisome and disconsolate thoughts which are often my lot in life, as those who have been kind enough to read me have surely been able to ascertain. From that moment on, I felt deprived of what optimists refer to as free will. My pig of a guardian angel towered over me with all of the ferocity of his virtue. He steered me along like a lamb garnished with a ribbon around its neck and, without speaking, he imposed upon me the tough, rudimentary truths of his wisdom. Through a fairly common phenomenon known as thought transference, he was communicating to me his personal vision of the landscape that surrounded us: the last roses brought in from Provins were transforming into Brussels sprouts; the trees, likely terrorized by the presence of my mentor, were sweating grease, and the sheep who made their way along the riverbank could feel their shanks sacrificing themselves for the common good. The meadows and woods were no longer populated by anything but boneless quadrupeds and birds. That strange sacrifice of the flora and fauna was coming to pass without pointless whining or unnecessarily abstract discussion. The many beasts of the great dietary college had taken their mission to heart.

"Three hundred and sixty pounds," and "no bones," bleated the sheep. The cattle were in agreement and the piglets too, naturally. Well, now! This abominable yet angelic spectacle turned my stomach embarrassingly. With an unconscious movement, I lit my pipe, no longer concerning myself with

my angel, and I went back into my abode. I made my way into the kitchen, where the water for the evening's soup was simmering away on the fire.

I was unable to suppress a sigh, the unexpected echo of which came straight back to me. With a start I turned and saw my angel. Without the least trace of surprise, I recognized Père Barbançon. His attitude, from his head down to his toes, had the unmistakable odor of a sermon, of that unforgiving sermon which leaves the most obstinate of sinners weak in the knees and in the voice.

Rage, that terrible counselor, poured into me like a ground swell. I took Barbançon by the throat and heaved him into the simmering stew. What ghastly soup! He was boneless, quite naturally, and meatless, too. I drank down a bit of that reprehensible decoction: it brought to mind printer's ink, the schools of my youth, radish broth, fresh candle drippings, and sewer lanterns.

That beneficent murder calmed the slightly aggressive hypochondria that had ruled over the nights and days of my existence. Père Barbançon, dead, freed me of certain worries. In a token gesture of recognition, I placed his tombstone next to those of Captain Hartmann and Lia. By carrying out this homicidal although purely literary gesture, it seemed to me that everything had ended well for me and that I too would be able to sleep easy . . .

from three to seven in the morning. That is the time of the night and the dawn that remains favorable to oblivion. The settling of nocturnal accounts, which are nothing but sterile enumerations of long-past experiences, naturally fades away within the unexplored landscape that is deep sleep.

Those who sleep like the proverbial log are not at all elegant. That sort of sleep is as unlyrical as can be. It is comparable to death, which, in spite of the fact that it comes to us all, is a nasty phenomenon and a revolting word.

EPILOGUE

I

A disagreeable uncertainty is still tormenting me, and has been ever since the more or less definitive passing of Père Barbançon. His many by-products trailed behind the funeral procession and the wind swept up the whole of it in swirling eddies of dead pages.

Was I mistaken about the final circumstances that gave the death of that fragile and tenacious felt puppet, well stitched though he was, a semblance of salutary authenticity? I find myself beset with doubts and my rest has been slightly diminished for it. As I write these words, Père Barbançon's shadow lurks in the background of every sheet of pulp paper I use. Completely transparent, not unlike a man of the sea who has been rendered sponge-like by decades of navigation, he is sitting down, contemplative, conniving, ready to meddle in anything and everything that in no way concerns him.

He's an interloper stuffed full of cypress sawdust, an interstellar troublemaker, a Cartesian devil floating in the sea, a too-tardy message in a bottle, although unfortunately not from very long ago. We know all about those pretty tubes of glass or pottery used by seamen as envelopes for the confidential messages they needed to get into the hands of the Administration of Currents and Tides. Père Barbançon, quite well informed about the various items used by the navy, those made of both wood and glass, must have made use of such objects, as inclined as he was to entrust his confidences to the good will of the four elements.

I don't think I would be too far off the mark if I were to suggest that Père Barbançon would have chosen a bottle that was of an appropriate size to contain him so that he could give himself over to the hospitality of some ocean or other, an act which would purge any authority from the felt figurine I keep at home, and which now seems like nothing more than a jovial misunderstanding, albeit an amusing one.

II

I have not entirely revealed all I know about Père Barbançon's character.

When he was active during a period of prosperity, Père Barbançon was fine with revealing himself to be pedantic and pompous. Furthermore, it could be said that he belonged to that category of people who, in Molière's day, were called the obstinates. Being obstinate was like a game for Barbançon. Without the least bit of difficulty, I can picture him dressed up like a clergyman so as to follow his own burial, or flat out refusing to participate in that sanitary service. Was it not in Bruges, in 19 . . . , that I had caught a glimpse, in the green and gray courtyard of a beguine monastery, of that aged joker gaily suspended from the bell rope they had used to signal mass? Which is proof of his ephemeral amiability. Depending on his mood, he would take up the shafts of an overladen cart or carry the mesh bag of a maid who was working up a sweat.

It takes me no effort at all to mentally reconstruct Barbançon, more commonly known as Père, dressed up in ceremonial regalia, evidently borrowed, decorated by multicolored medals of honor, as he goes off to join our little family, trailing behind his own mortal remains.

I know all too well that every man in good health dies four times. There is the death of the child, that of the adolescent, that of the grown man and that of the geriatric. Only this last can be counted as the fourth.

Père Barbançon was a great collector of different deaths. He lived on in order to perpetuate his innate proclivity for harassing his contemporaries. I think it would be nearly impossible to write the funeral oration of such a man without dedicating your life to the task. And there can be no question of sacrificing one's existence to such a poorly remunerative labor.

III

There is a little house located between Mobile and Galveston that Guillaume Apollinaire mentions in one of his poems. It would work very well as the setting for the logical and more or less moral end of our adventurer. It was inside a kind of coal storage shed, furnished with a few shovels and a battered barrel, that Père Barbançon finally took his liftoff toward eternity, which Malherbe once described as "making one's fortune equivalent with immortality."

Despite the overuse of the cowboy in recent times, a recurrent device so often inflicted upon us within the lyricism of the picturesque, I find it difficult not to indicate the presence of a few of those boys, those mounted righters-of-the-wrong of the cavalry, by the rose-bedecked door of that death chamber.

The hanging of Père Barbançon will, as a final reading, lend to these remembrances a moral conclusion that might seem in some ways to be lacking. This is not so much a question of principle, which is debatable, but rather a question about the hanging itself, the act that has borne out this task. Nor is it with a pitiful cord fashioned of rolled sheets of paper that one might obtain such a result.

In Père Barbançon's time, rope was of high quality, and the sun, which forced its way into the tragic slums of that ignored corner of Texas, could still illuminate the smallest of details, such as the hanging of this horseman of the Apocalypse according to the ingratiating mode of expressive translation in use among those who collect anxieties.

The difficulty, of course, was to reckon in which capacity our Padre Barbançon would be hanged. As a good-for-nothing? A professor of transcendental hypocrisy? For academic merit? Because of his role as False Face, the wearer of masks? As traitor to a dynamic equilibrium? In memory of Bambù and her clique? In homage to God knows what spirit of somewhat confused justice? What a story!

IV

At different times in my life—although this time, having donned a tweed suit of armor, cut to measure—I revisited the various landscapes that served as ornamentation for the indefatigable activity of Père Barbançon. That old-timer flitted about among the clouds. He seemed to float in the sky like a once-captive balloon that had found its independence thanks to a breach of contract between it and the ground. Barbançon's celestial lightness, which had little to do with his weight, was not at all surprising. His destiny, in the accessible spheres of aerostatic metaphysics, was flighty, light-heart-ed, irresolute, capricious, innocent. Loosed from the grape-bunch of col-ored balloons with which children amuse themselves, he possessed that lightweight obesity that we can effortlessly admire as it bounces on the end of an indulgent length of string. Those who confuse the old-fashioned, an-imal-fabricated red balloons with souls soaring off on their way to purga-tory are not as bereft of resources as they seem. Those souls bounce back at the least nudge from the finger of God.

As for weighty souls, those which do not bounce back at the least nudge, among those of the divine realm, they become the balls of cold iron which make it possible to shackle the enslaved to their habits. Outside of all theology, unless it is that of the penal colony, they are called *manacles*, which, although derived from the Latin for hand, might lead our minds to take the word more personally. These iron bracelets are attached to the chain that is riveted to the ball, without which the ball would serve no purpose.

Many times I have seen Père Barbançon dragging one of his legs be-hind him like someone who used to wear manacles. It is that memory, which Vidocq has helped me to define, that gives me the impression of the amazing lightness of Barbançon's soul, whose lack of consistency never ceases to impose itself upon any and all exercises in preparation for that fi-nal, permanent experience.

V

And it is thus that, being subjected to the fantasies of a progressive melancholia, we reach the final image that must bring this series of funereal orations to a close. And so, to you who have suffered, perhaps unbeknownst to him, here lies Père Barbançon on his deathbed. His face, now at rest, no longer reveals anything picturesque. An appeased face, as smooth as a fresh page at the beginning of what will perhaps end up a book.

Père Barbançon has been reduced to the common denominator. No longer anything more than any other detail of the life of a society. He is shielded from all vengeance, and can slumber without letting himself be tormented by the sound of footsteps in a stairwell that leads into the shadowy world of his nocturnal activities. In a sleep as rigid as marble, the romantic charms of the life of a rogue permanently fade into oblivion.

This sad character has yielded his place. And the adventures of which he was the architect are no longer those of Père Barbançon, who, formerly full of life, is now genuinely dead against his will. And so the often imaginary animator of this chronicle, with a final word that turns the key on this final chapter, rejoins Signorina Bambù, and Captain Hartmann, a man who also sought to guarantee the tranquility of his final rest. As has been said in the first part of this remembrance.

1948

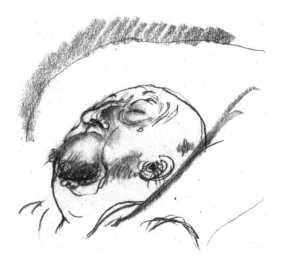

GUS BOFA IN THE SHADOWS OF LITERATURE

When Gus Bofa died in 1968, his obituary in *Le nouveau planète* described him as "a profound thinker . . . a bilingual philosopher who knew how to tell us about fear in words and images."[1] Bofa's drawings indeed evoke the anxious spirit of the early twentieth century, images of urban alienation and war but also of fantasy, a mixture he shared with his friend Pierre Mac Orlan. Words, either Bofa's or others, are central to his oeuvre. His drawings suggest the existential darkness that overtook Europe defaced by war and modernization. The illustrations he made for Mac Orlan's *Mademoiselle Bambù*—of spies, prostitutes, sailors, and drifters—appear in a rough black and white, sketch-like, as if somehow disappearing into themselves. In these drawings, his style is dark, almost resembling the aesthetics of film noir, even if at times goofy or playful.

Bofa himself has become as obscure as the shadowy figures that populate his drawings. Some of that is due to the fact that during his lifetime, he preferred to avoid fame and remained instead on the edges of public life. Another is the marginal role that a book illustrator receives in literary history. A minor revival has occurred in France, where his books are now collector's items, particularly because of his influence on *bande dessiné*. In 2000, thirty-two years after his death, an exhibition about the collaborations between him and Pierre Mac Orlan was mounted at Musée de l'Abbaye de Sainte Croix aux Sables d'Olonne. Throughout the last decade, Éditions Cornélius has reprinted a number of his books, as well as published a biography of him by Emmanuel Pollaud-Dulian in 2013. Although at first glance Bofa's work exists in the tidal zone between French political cartoons of the nineteenth century and the *bande dessiné* of the twentieth, on closer scrutiny it is more in spirit with modernist literature, something highlighted in his collaborations with Mac Orlan.

Born Gustave Blanchot in 1883, Bofa was drawn to visual art and writing from an early age. He grew up in Bordeaux until his father, a military officer, moved the family to Paris, where the young boy finished his schooling. Around the time of the family's move, Bofa started signing his childhood works with only initials, which he claimed stood for "Gus Bofa." The name suggests boyish mischief: *gus* can mean "rascal" in Niçoise dialect, which Emmanuel Pollaud-Dulian suggests that his mother may have spoken and thus Bofa may have heard as a child, while the phrase *faire un bofa* can mean "to be a failure."[2] After his education, Bofa focused his attention on visual arts, although he still read copiously. At seventeen, after knocking on the front door of the editor of *Sourire*, Bofa began drawing for that weekly, still up to mischief by signing his name "G. Bofa." Apparently the name had stuck. By 1909, *Le Figaro* was describing Bofa as a "master."[3] That same year he also took on an editorial position at the low-brow illustrated weekly *Le Rire*.[4]

During the First World War, Bofa continued to further his reputation as an illustrator. For *La Baïonnette*, he drew satirical images of the front, where he was stationed until discharged with an injury.[5] His drawings are frank, without concealing the brutality of war or its effects on soldiers. Afterward, he started publishing short books of illustrations with text, some written by him, such as *Slogans* and *Synthèse Littéraires et Anti-Littéraires*. *Slogans*, for example, paired often-ironic aphorisms about human nature with comedic sketches, while *Synthèse* contained portraits of writers and other notables. He also started illustrating books, for which he would become best known.

Since his revival, Bofa's influence on illustration in France has been well documented. Yet his importance in the history of literature is less accounted for. *Bande dessiné*, as we now know it, did not exist when Bofa was making his most important work.[6] Although significant, his association with BD has now overshadowed other aspects of his oeuvre. If not a "writer" of a sort, Bofa is, at least, a modern artist whose sensibility constantly crosses the boundaries between the visual and verbal arts in unique ways. His drawings offer a different meaning to the dubious term "paraliterary"—a word that has, for other reasons, unfairly haunted the reputation of Pierre Mac Orlan as well. As an editor, writer, and illustrator, Bofa stands at a crossroads between numerous art forms: book illustration, comics, poster art, aphorisms, and visual biography. These kinds of mixings and his emphasis on mass-produced art were elements of Bofa's modernism. His long-standing collaborations with Pierre Mac Orlan, on a variety of projects, extended those sensibilities. Mac Orlan described Bofa as the best illustrator for Mac Orlan's term "the social fantastic," while Bofa once claimed that the two of them were so in synch that Bofa could draw illustrations at the same time that Mac Orlan wrote.[7] Bofa's statement implies that his contributions were also collaborations in a more complicated sense.

An avid reader throughout his life, in the 1920s and 1930s, Bofa also penned book reviews for *Le Crapouillot*, including writings on André Gide, Ernest Hemingway, William Faulkner, Louis-Ferdinand Céline, and Blaise Cendrars. While Bofa's literary criticism hardly amounts to either a staggering output or a particularly remarkable one (and they have the misfortune of having been published in a magazine that veered to the extreme right in the postwar period), his reviews indicate sympathy for modernist writing, even when he was critical of it, in the case of Faulkner's *Sartoris*, or in Bofa's critique of Gide's Soviet sympathies.[8] More importantly, during this same period, Bofa became renowned for illustrated editions of literary classics—Thomas de Quincey's *On Murder Considered as One of the Fine Arts*, Swift's *Gulliver's Travels*, Baudelaire's translations of Poe, and Cervantes's *Don Quixote*. Among them, Bofa's brightly colored *Quixote* is considered his masterpiece of book illustration.[9]

Much like the way he chose to keep a nickname that he had given himself when young, throughout Bofa's oeuvre the childlike nature of many of his illustrations walks side by side with a very adult fear, such as the goofy cartoon-like rendering of Pére Barbançon—who, in one illustration, is depicted hanging from a noose. A morbid imagination runs deep in Bofa, one that somehow remains tied to both childhood and the nightmares of the twentieth century. As a boy, he set up a make-believe graveyard in his family's garden, where he would hold pretend funerals for all family members, even their cat.[10] In terms of his process, Bofa's drawings often began in an odd way: Throughout his life, he made puppets that he modeled his figures on. They are strange, creepy-looking things. It's almost as if his drawings originate from monsters. In both words and image, the fear is here. As Mac Orlan wrote in *Le quai des brumes*, "All of us possess, deep in the dark night of our thoughts, an abattoir that reeks."[11]

NOTES

1. Claude Vallée, quoted in Emmanuel Pollaud-Dulian, *Gus Bofa: L'enchanteur désenchanté* (Bordeaux: Éditions Cornélius, 2013), 520. (Translation mine.)

2. Pollaud-Dulian, *Gus Bofa*, 19.

3. Ibid., 52.

4. Benoît Decron, "Gus Bofa (1883–1968): Les plaies de l'ombre," in *Gus Bofa et Mac Orlan* (Saint-Cry-sur-Morin: Musée de l'Abbaye de Sainte Croix aux Sables d'Olonne, 2000), 42.

5. Ibid, 43.

6. The term *bande dessiné* was coined in 1938 although it does not gain popular usage until the 1950s. From Erwann Tancé, "La (presque) véritable histoire des mots 'bande dessinée,'" *Comixtrip.fr* (accessed 4 August 2017), http://www.comixtrip.fr/dossiers/la-presque-verita-ble-histoire-des-mots-bande-dessinee/.

7. Pollaud-Dulian, *Gus Bofa*, 453–454.

8. Gus Bofa, "Gus Bofa Critiques Litteraire," Gusbofa.com (accessed 4 August 2017), http://www.gusbofa.com/critique.php3.

9. Pollaud-Dulian, *Gus Bofa*, 284.

10. Ibid., 13.

11. Pierre Mac Orlan, *Le quai des brumes* (Paris: Gallimard, 1927), 69. (Translation mine.)

Chris Clarke's translations include work by Oulipo members Raymond Queneau (New Directions) and François Caradec (MIT Press). He received a PEN/Heim Translation Fund Grant in 2016 for his translation of Marcel Schwob's *Imaginary Lives* (Wakefield Press), and his translation of Patrick Modiano's *In the Café of Lost Youth* (NYRB Classics) was shortlisted for the 2016 French-American Foundation Translation Prize.

Aaron Peck is the author of a novel, *The Bewilderments of Bernard Willis*, and a monograph, *Jeff Wall: North & West*. His art criticism frequently appears in *Artforum*.